Copyright © 2022 by Brennan LaFaro
Cover Art © 2022 by Donnie Goodman

First published in 2022 by DarkLit Press
Edited by Kelly Brockelhurst

ISBN 978-1-7386585-1-0

PRAISE FOR NOOSE

"LaFaro's *Noose* is a bloodbath of a tale of the Olde West, where violence and vengeance are bought and sold at the General Store and skeletons are buried in the back yard. Burning with loneliness and small-town insularity, *Noose* is a chilling addition to the western horror genre. A vicious ear-worm that will keep you humming long after you put the book down."

—Lee Murray, USA Today Bestselling Author and four-time Bram Stoker Award®-winner.

"*Noose* is a gritty yarn of strange violence and loss, of regret and brutal revenge, with dark blood running through its twisted heart. I love a weird western and this is a damn good one."

— Alan Baxter, award-winning author of *Sallow Bend* and *The Gulp*

"Like a bullet from a gun, Brennan LaFaro's *Noose* comes screaming off the pages. A blood-soaked western with assassins waiting around every corner, this darkly funny adventure crackles with energy."

— Tyler Jones, author of *Criterium* and *Almost Ruth*

BOOKS BY
BRENNAN LAFARO

Slattery Falls
Decimated Dreams

NOOSE

BRENNAN LAFARO

DARKLIT
PRESS

CONTENT WARNING

The story that follows may contain
graphic violence and gore.

Please go to the very back of the book
for more detailed content warnings.

Beware of spoilers.

For Dustin,

Who helped me breathe life into Noose's gang.
This one's for you,
partner.

CONTENTS

Authors Note

The town of Buzzard's Edge is totally fictional. Although these stories take place in mid-to-late 1800s Arizona, and I do reference local wildlife, flora and fauna, places, and natural fixtures, I've taken some liberties with the geography, as a writer of fiction does. I hope you enjoy it anyway.

CHAPTER 1

I FEEL LIKE A MORNING STAR

The first time I ever met George "Noose" Holcomb, I knew that someday I'd kill him. Either that or he'd finish what he started during the Buzzard's Edge train robbery of 1872. That day my family boarded an engine supposedly so damn fast it should have left any unwanted company, and the horse it rode in on, in the dust.

But that's not what happened.

Noose pulled up alongside the passenger car on a sleek black stallion with glowing red eyes. Famine was the horse's name, existing only to take without mercy from those who laid eyes on it. A creature born of evil, or perhaps made that way by man. Or woman. One of those stories nobody ever seemed to tell, but everybody knew.

The horse galloped faster than it had any right to, as if it had a mind to outrun the devil himself, but the passengers knew better. The real devil rode on the back of that horse, leaning forward and paying no mind to the blanched faces watching him overtake their expensive and state-of-the-art train. Before the guard suspected a thing, the man was on board. Iron filled each hand as Famine fell back to wait for orders. Wide eyes and gaping mouths greeted his arrival. Despite the absence of his gang of ruffians, nobody on that train doubted which notorious outlaw stood before them, casting an ominous shadow through the rumbling passenger car.

Difficult as it was to tear my eyes from the monster before me, I watched the horse fade against the horizon. It made no effort to keep in stride with the train. Even my eight-year-old mind understood this guy had no plans to grab and go. Holcomb would bring this train to its metaphorical knees.

Noose dominated the front of the car, his broad shoulders filling the aisle. He wore a gray jacket and matching wool pants. Whether he fought alongside the confederates or killed one and stole their uniform depended on the person who spread the rumor. His midnight black, wide-brimmed hat threw a shadow over his face, one that almost, but didn't quite, cover the scar running the length of his neck. A reminder of the time Buzzard's Edge tried to hang him, but didn't quite pull it off. That story never changed when people told it. Too many witnesses.

The passengers watched in frozen terror, distinguishable from a display of statues only by their ragged breathing and faint whimpers. The class of people returning to Buzzard's Edge had heard tell of outlaws such as this, but didn't believe them. Or at least tried to ignore them. The kids knew the actual stories, the ones worth sharing in the dark. These sheltered civilians spent more than a few shield nickels to keep that barrier between the center of Buzzard's Edge and the wild outskirts, as well as themselves, alive. From the first sighting of the obsidian horse to Noose lording over the aisle and eye-fucking the purses, wallets, and watches, only half a minute had passed.

A gunshot shattered the panicked silence. The richest citizens of Buzzard's Edge all clutched their chests, searching for a bullet hole, displaying such synchronicity as to make the movement appear practiced. A tangible wave of relief rolled through the car when the hired guard charged forth from the far end of the train. His rifle continued to smoke, taking responsibility for the initial shot. Hunkered down in anticipation of return fire, the guard squeezed off a second round straight at Noose Holcomb.

The bullet tore through Holcomb's shirt, leaving singed edges to border an unmarred patch of chest. A collective gasp filled the coach as Noose lowered his head to inspect the damage— or lack thereof—his brim covering his weathered face and, for a moment, that hideous scar. When his head swung back up, the trace of a smile had taken up residence. A naive fool might mistake the smile for mirth and humor, but a quick glance at the man's eyes told a different story.

Greed and hate.

Holcomb lifted his revolver in a blur and squeezed the trigger to make it scream. The shot rang through the car, denying the penitent guard so much as a moment to regain his composure. His melon burst beneath his cap, staining the wall behind him in a mess of crimson.

Shrieks traveled from all corners of the car as the body dropped, still twitching. A full-fledged smile danced onto Noose's hellscape of a face. Shit-eating grin and all, he withdrew a burlap sack from behind his back and waved it in the air.

"Now listen he-ah, listen he-ah," he intoned, sounding not unlike the traveling preachers that occasionally made their way through town. Daddy always said not to trust them either. "Unless you fine folks care to join this gentleman in discovering what it feels like to have a bullet pass through your skull, I'll be requiring anything of value you have on your person."

When silence met his declaration, he cocked one eyebrow and continued. "Well, hell. I guess money don't buy brains."

Throughout the lecture, he'd allowed the gun to drape lazily by his side. Rapid as a rattlesnake strike, he raised it to chest height. A crack sounded and the older woman sitting across the aisle from me gasped. The sharp intake of breath startled me nearly as much as the shot. Scarlet bloomed on the front of her shirt as her wheezing gathered speed. The fifth and sixth gulps failed to pull in more air. Her face displayed a rictus so pained, her eyeballs bulged, seeking egress. After a few more attempts to draw breath into her ruined lungs, she slumped in her seat, still and silent.

Holcomb's hearty voice filled the cabin, uncontested.

"If y'all don't think I got enough bullets to do that to each and every one of you, you are both sorry and mistaken." He paused for a moment, allowing the mental imagery to set in. "Now, when I said anything of value, clearly I spoke over your heads, so I shan't do so again. Give me your shiny shit. Watches, coins, necklaces, rings. If it sparkles, it goes in the bag."

He scanned the stupid, bovine faces. The car bustled with activity as passengers removed any detachable shiny objects and prepared to make their offering. Holcomb's grin, still in place from before he shot that woman, crept closer toward his ears.

He sauntered down the aisle holding the bag wide, relishing the clinks and tinkles the metal made as it collected at the bottom of his bountiful sack. Whistling a carefree melody, he paused next to my seat and finished the chorus.

"Know that tune, boy?"

I nodded, my eyes fixed on the dead woman seated across the aisle. My heart still held out a smidge of hope that her chest might hitch and she'd start laughing, the whole thing a joke. Noose followed my gaze to the dead woman and brayed like it was the funniest damn thing he ever saw. Even slapped his knee.

"Shoo fly, don't bother me. For I belong to somebody," he crooned in a toneless voice. People who sang like that usually reeked of whiskey, but not Noose Holcomb. He stank of moist earth. It reminded me of when the town came together to bury Grandpa. A fresh pile of dirt towered over the hole in the ground, but it wasn't the kind you wanted to play in.

Confusion and fear overwhelmed my small body. Unsure of what the man expected, I began singing, the words leaving my mouth before I could stop them. I used to sing sometimes during my piano lessons with Momma. She always said I had the voice of an angel, but one who hid in the back of the choir. "I feel, I feel, I feel like a morning star." Solo on the first line of the chorus, but with that maniacal, out-of-tune accompaniment on the second. Wet warmth streamed down my face as I finished the line.

Momma wrapped her arm tighter around my shoulders, her bright turquoise dress unmistakable from the corner of my eye. She always dressed so nicely, even at home with nobody to impress. The way she shook made me believe she feared misspeaking. Daddy didn't have that problem.

Tossing the family's valuables into the open sack, he said, "You have what you came for; now leave us alone. Can't you see he's scared?" The admonishment contained a bit more vinegar than Daddy probably meant to put in there. He'd always taught me to speak kindly to people. It was a shame his last words contained something of a rough edge.

Noose never even looked at William Daggett. He locked eyes with me while singing and held my gaze even as he lifted the revolver and blew the back of Daddy's head through the glass and all over the landscape whizzing by. Momma screamed, a sound beyond compare. Even fifteen years later, I can't summon the description to do it justice. I heard her heart break, knowing the man she'd loved was dead, and that her only son was up next.

The scream demanded Holcomb's attention, and not a moment too soon. By then, I would've sold my soul to avoid one more second of staring into that man's fiery eyes. He discharged his revolver right into Mae Daggett's open mouth, abruptly silencing her cries. The top of her head vanished. It didn't go out the window or back into the next seat. It was just gone.

I didn't make a peep. Didn't have time before the gun seized its sights on me. Noose held the barrel under my chin and leaned in, the stench of grave dirt digging its claws in. The rest of the train tried to listen in as Holcomb whispered in my ear. "I ain't gonna kill you, boy, on account of you shared a song with me. But I could. I've got two bullets left in the chamber here. There's about twelve people left in this train car. Twelve. Ain't one of 'em trying to stop me right now." He pulled back and met my eyes again, nodded, then continued. "Y'all think I'm the bad guy, and you ain't wrong, but I'm hardly alone. And you won't find me cryin' over what I done today."

Noose removed the gun from my throat and started reloading, slow and methodical, as if he had all the time in the world. Even filled with fury and not thinking straight, I couldn't disagree with the sentiment. I was the only person under thirty on that train and not one of the fuckin' cowards risked their own skin to try and save me. Around the car, about a dozen pairs of eyes studied the ceiling, the floor, and the passing landscape. Noose loaded the sixth round into the cylinder, gave it a spin, and closed it. The metallic clicking diminished, then disappeared, leaving the train in silence. Even the chugging engine barely registered in the background. "What's your name, shoo fly?"

"Rory Daggett," I stammered out, thinking to add something tough, like telling him to remember it, but the first four syllables proved trouble enough to get out.

"Not a bad moniker, as far as those things go. You remember what I said, kid." A cloud shifted over his face, one of the rare times during that robbery he didn't make light of the situation. "Until we meet again." He returned to his feet and continued collecting loot. When he'd reached the last sucker, Noose gave the bag a twist and let it drop to the floor. Hundreds, if not thousands, of dollars' worth of extraneous shit these people would never miss clinked as it hit the thin carpet.

Holcomb reached behind his back and removed a second gun. Holding them both at shoulder-level, that familiar devil's grin returned to his face. He might've laughed, but I'd never know. Understanding what came next, I covered my ears and ducked as Noose unleashed demonic fury throughout the cabin. Shrapnel struck, pelting me from all sides, whether parts of the seats blown apart or chunks of human tissue, I couldn't be sure. Even when I chanced it being safe to open my eyes, blood and bone littered the aisles so generously, I knew the gore must have covered me like a blanket.

The firestorm ceased and the silence returned, somehow heavier than before, until Noose broke it.

". . . ten, eleven. What do you know, shoo fly?" he asked as I uncovered my ears. "I guessed twelve left breathing and counting you, that's exactly what we got. Means I got one bullet left in here. Think I should give it to the engineer or save it for a special occasion?"

"I… I don't know how to drive a train." The only reply my traumatized mind could come up with.

"No, I don't suppose you do. And if I leave you to die out here in the middle of nowhere on a broken-down engine, I don't suppose Buzzard's Edge gets the message I want to send. So how 'bout it? You up to deliver a message?"

I nodded eagerly, afraid anything less than unbridled enthusiasm would make Noose change his mind about the location of that bullet. Holcomb replaced one revolver back in its holster, then snapped open the cylinder of the other. He dumped the last bullet into his open palm, then pinched it between a filthy thumb and forefinger. Holding it out, he didn't utter a word. Simply waited for me to take it.

I did.

As Holcomb turned toward the door he came in through, I squeezed the bullet as hard as I could, like if I crushed it with enough force, the outlaw might feel the same pain he'd inflicted. Even just a little. But if Noose felt anything at all, he sure as hell didn't show it.

Famine galloped alongside the passenger windows. Holcomb hadn't signaled for him, but the steed came anyway, and its rider mounted, making the transfer at a frightening speed. Together, they disappeared.

In the center of the abattoir, I allowed the tears to fall. I wailed. It was another twenty-five minutes before the train arrived at the station and the driver, tucked away up front next to the noisy engine, discovered what had become of his cargo.

CHAPTER 2

CRIMSON MIST

Ghost's hooves beat the ground with the resonance and steady pulse of a bass drum. The tempo screeched along like a marching band being chased by the armies of hell. Six years ago, when I found this feral mare wandering out behind Taff Ranch, I couldn't even hope to climb on her black-and-white spotted back, never mind tell her what to do. These days, we practically read each other's minds. With the slightest tug on one of the reins, she took any curve the desert could offer, no matter how tight.

Crane's horse, every bit as sleek but with shorter legs, huffed and puffed, trying to outrun us, but never stood a chance. A smile spread across my face knowing full fucking well that Ghost was just toying with them.

Weaving through rocky outcrops and kicking up clouds of sand, Ghost closed the gap with ease, eventually herding Crane's smoky gray gelding into an inlet we both knew didn't have an outlet. Before I could pull back on the reins, Ghost let up on the throttle, skidding to a stop just before the rocks opened up to expose us. A handful of pebbles skittered into the mouth of the inlet, the shimmering sound giving way to a troubling silence.

Crane's horse had stopped as well.

Keeping any noise that might give us away to a minimum, I dismounted. My hand found my trusty six-shooter, a gift from Henry Taff on my seventeenth birthday. I didn't bother to check the ammo. It would be full. No sense chasing after a shitbag of this magnitude unless you're ready to let the bullets fly at a moment's notice.

We'd chased him down for a simple enough reason, on the surface anyway: robbing the Buzzard's Edge First Bank. It happened at least a couple times a year, and typically Sheriff Harden was up to the task—a good man, if a little constrained by the forces of law and order—but we'd heard rumors of Crane hitting the banks in Dusty Streams and Tucson. He didn't play fair, and it seemed some of that knowledge got into my horse, for she wasn't about to poke her head around that corner.

That wasn't the first time I'd heard Crane's name, however. It originally drew my attention riding on the tail of another name, one I listened for like a hawk in pursuit of a quick meal.

Noose Holcomb.

Crane earned his reputation dabbling in the sciences, though not the kind they taught in schoolhouses. He then became a key component of Noose's gang, one conspicuously absent the day of the train robbery.

There was a time, Harden would say, when a man walked into the bank and tossed a bag across the desk. He might jam a pistol in someone's face if the implied threat didn't do the trick, but there was some honor in playing to expectations. They'd string those robbers up just the same, of course—make 'em dance until they went blue in the face—but there were no hard feelings, if you can believe that.

Word was Crane walked into the Dusty Streams bank, no mask and no firearm. Instead, he plucked a vial from his belt, containing something so bright blue it made water look lifeless. He held it aloft like everyone ought to be impressed, then unscrewed the lid, tossed it over the counter, and took a few steps back.

The teller, a young woman not much older than me, shot him a confused look, then started itching at her face. A little at first, then more frantic until she tore patches from her cheeks, digging deep gouges. I didn't see it with my own eyes, but witnesses said you could see her teeth, though she sure as hell wasn't smiling.

The guards, noticing the woman's frenzy, approached with pistols drawn. Crane gave them no reason to suspect him of any malfeasance, so they passed him by. As soon as they reached the banker's station, they joined her in trying to get rid of that pesky skin. Screams of agony cut through the bank's stifled air as the employees and eventually, other customers, peeled the flesh from their faces, from their arms and chests, as well. Unable to bear it, yet unable to stop.

Blood coated the hardwood floor, so thick I'm told, you couldn't walk from one side of the building to the other without slipping and falling on your ass, ruining your best pair of pants. The scene made my stomach turn. Especially the part with him stepping over those mutilated corpses like they were horse apples in the road, all to help himself to a little cash.

As soon as Crane showed up in Buzzard's Edge, he made straight for the bank. I hadn't yet received report of the damage he'd done, but I feared it would line up with the first account. Or possibly it would be worse.

Harden had stopped by the ranch on the way to the bank, excitement gleaming in his eyes. It'd been years since one of the names on my list surfaced, leading me to believe they might never. The sheriff would do sheriff things, calm down the survivors while I tracked down the escaped outlaw. I'd meet up with Harden later at Lynch's Tavern, get all the details, assuming Crane didn't get a chance to use that concoction on me. I didn't fancy riding back into town with no skin on my face.

I knelt to pick up a stone, hoping my knees wouldn't crack like cannons and betray my position. Showing their loyalty in silence, they held my weight as I chucked the stone. No bullets came and that was alright, because I didn't expect they would. Not his style. Instead, a small glass vial flew out from the alcove, cracking open on the hard-packed desert floor. The tinkling of glass pervaded the air, followed by a dark red mist. The unnatural sight of it rising into the clear afternoon made me shiver despite the heat.

I jumped back, dragging Ghost by my side, and covered my mouth and nose with the bandana I kept draped around my neck. It wasn't much, but I prayed to the Lord above it would suffice.

The mist dissolved in the air, lost to the blazing blue sky, and left only the remnants of glass and a curious scrabbling noise behind. I recognized it as the sound of a desperate man abandoning his horse and trying to scale sheer rock face to find freedom above. I listened intently, in part to keep apprised of any progress he might make, but also because I didn't trust whatever heinous mixture he'd tossed my way to be gone yet. Let the fucker tire himself out, I figured.

It didn't take long before the frantic pawing became labored breathing.

A man of science stood little chance against the natural obstacles of the Sonoran Desert, and judging by the sound— or sudden lack thereof—he'd exhausted himself. Now if the name I sought to cross off my list was Dorrance, this might have gone in a multitude of directions, but I'd studied up on Crane's history enough to make some naive predictions regarding what he'd do next.

An idea occurred. An incredibly reckless one, probably, but it was all I had. Securing the bandana around my mouth—a fool's hope for the world's biggest fool—I removed my hat and crept toward the opening. Eyes wide open and body ready to spring, I'd only get one chance at this.

"Drop everything, you cur!" I shouted, springing into view. My first clear look at Crane revealed his back pressed to the steep rock face like a cornered animal. His wanted posters described him as six-foot-five and they didn't exaggerate. The tall, thin man allowed a trace of panic to impose itself on his features, before a cunning conceit took its place. As I suspected, no gun made an appearance, and I cursed myself for an idiot, because the momentary panic would have afforded me enough time to shoot him where he stood. Yet my revolver remained safely holstered, my hands filled with a harmless hat. I expect he thought I'd come begging for my supper.

One moment he stood empty-handed, the next he produced another vial, as if by magic. He wound up to throw the small glass cylinder, lit up an unearthly dark, glowing red. Bottled malevolence. I positioned myself where the first one had smashed, but this throw came up short. Hat outstretched, I dove forward and felt the most insignificant of weights drop into the center of the hat with a soft whoosh. No crack, no tinkle telling the story of broken glass and unleashed toxin. I trusted my ears and didn't check, figuring I'd be just as dead by some horrible means if I confirmed a leak.

Laying on my stomach all the while—decidedly not part of the plan—I snatched the vial and sent it careening toward Crane's head. His eyes shot open in shock and a temporary paralysis took over that allowed it to sail right by his gaping mouth, smashing to bits only inches away from him.

I clambered to my feet, taking a few steps back. He underwent no physical transformation. Any thoughts I had of boils erupting on his skin, projectile vomiting blood, or any other grotesqueries from the wilds of my imagination, fled. The only part of him that moved was his eyes. Already open to what I considered capacity, his eyelids peeled back further. The creak of stretched leather as they wound back wouldn't have sounded out of place. Crane's sudden gaunt and haggard appearance told of a man who had seen death and lived to tell about it, but not for very long.

When his eyes reached the point where they risked spilling from his head, his mouth opened to scream in sympathy. The inhuman shrieks that escaped more closely resembled a choir trapped inside a burning church than the panicked man before me. The sustained scream held its pitch for a moment, maybe two, then began to degrade as though a knife scraped down his vocal cords, whittling them away to ribbons. Whatever that vial contained, I thanked my lucky stars I hadn't caught a whiff.

Intermingled with Crane's pained cries were words, as confusing as they were unsettling.

"Demons!" he yelped, his voice dragging across gravel. "Tearing at my flesh! So many arms! Why so many arms? Help! Why aren't you helping?" His hands, previously engaged in batting away invisible monsters, latched onto the front of my shirt. Despite the proximity of our faces, he didn't see me. Not in any meaningful way. He pleaded, more with his tone than his words. That's when his legs failed him.

Crane sank to the ground with a muffled thud, his howls ceasing as he fell to the sand. His eyes remained open, but they saw little, if anything, of the surrounding world. Madness enveloped those eyes as they lit upon something the brain wasn't prepared for. The pupils fired back and forth as if studying words on a page, like he might be able to save his sanity if he could only read fast enough. I crouched next to the scientist, intent on questioning him no matter how little good it might do.

"Holcomb. When's the last time you saw him?"

His eyes continued their rapid movement, the rest of his face vacant, and any expectations I had of a competent answer flew the coop. I asked twice more, for all the good it did, and received only an occasional twitch of the lips, the eyes persisting in their fruitless search. Patting down his body, I found glass vials stored in the same manner most men stored their bullets, tucked carefully within pockets contained on his leather belt. More of the cloudy crimson mist that had driven Crane to the brink of insanity, the fabled bright blue from the Dusty Streams robbery, and an array of green, pink, and darkest black. I couldn't guess at what kind of chaos the final three might unleash if broken.

Against my better judgment, I reached for the belt on Crane's person to bring back to Buzzard's Edge. I couldn't very well leave it here for anyone to stumble on, and I couldn't destroy it not knowing the effects. I unclipped the belt and slowly pulled it from underneath the man. His hand shot forward, grabbing my wrist with its gnarled talons. My heart leapt in my chest and I damn near lost hold of the fragile glass. Steadying my breath, I turned toward his face, coming to rest on his eyes. They no longer darted from side to side, but met my own.

Unintelligible garbling spilled from his mouth. It took until the third repetition to make sense of the words. "Morning star." Said again and again. The hair stood up on the back of my arms. Now we were getting somewhere.

I gave Crane a shake, and he mumbled something like, "In the cavern. He waits in the cavern."

My heart rate steadied. My breathing slowed. The heat beat down from the Arizona sun, drawing sweat from my overexerted body, but all that cascaded to the back of my mind. I lifted him with my free hand.

"Who waits? Noose? What caverns?"

As it turned out, I had more questions than he had time.

The twitch at the corner of his mouth became a smile for the slightest instant, then went slack. Foam collected where his lips turned down and his pupils appeared as though they were about to resume their bouncing. Instead they ascended, rolling to the back of his head, leaving only the whites of his eyes. Crane's body mimicked the twitch at his mouth. What it lacked in length, it made up for in intensity. Intent on keeping the vials from damage, I dropped him to the ground, where he finished his flopping then lay still. His chest hitched once more, then deigned neither to rise or fall.

By his own creation, Simon Crane had met his maker.

CHAPTER 3

ANTS

"Just fuckin' keeled over?" Harden took a swig from his glass. The color in his cheeks betrayed the number of drinks he'd downed before I arrived. He caught the look I gave him. "Don't worry, hoss, I'm off duty. Billy's more'n capable of holding things down at the station. Besides, if trouble erupted, you ain't half in your cups yet."

I nodded. An oversimplified response to the sheriff's verbal diarrhea. "Will those . . . things be safe there?"

"The chemicals? I expect so. Locked up in a safe only me and Billy have the combination to, though anybody knows me well enough could probably guess it." He shot me a wink and I hoped to God he hadn't used his birthday, though part of me suspected that's exactly what he'd done.

"Fair enough."

"What happened to the horse?"

"Come again?"

"That lanky fucker took off from the bank like a bat out of hell, horse pounding down the main drag, and you only a few minutes behind him. He still have a horse when you caught up with him?"

"Oh, yeah. Poor thing was right next to him when the poison got released, whatever it was. I got Crane's body slumped over the back of Ghost. Went to grab his horse and lead it back with us, but I found it on the ground, foaming from the mouth."

"Left her there?" The lingering joviality abandoned Harden's demeanor. Even too-many-drinks deep, he recalled my affinity for horses.

Another nod. "Didn't have much of a choice, I guess. Hey, John?"

His eyes sobered. He knew what I had on my mind. "Don't know what the chemical was, but it left three dead at the bank. Wasn't the skin-tearing stuff we heard about. Don't think it was whatever got Crane either. I'll spare you the grisly details, Rory, but you ever been so sick you felt like you was gonna vomit 'til your innards turned to outards?"

"Sure," I said, not liking where this was going.

He held out splayed hands, no doubt intending to convey the end of the story so he didn't have to finish. He failed. Clearing his throat, Harden added, "Well, me too, but I've got to imagine that feeling pales in comparison to what these folks went through."

We drank in silence for a few minutes, neither of us having the words or the desire to continue that line of conversation.

"Another round, gentlemen?" If Emmett Lynch could smile, either with his face or his words, I'd never been privy to it. One would think being surrounded by booze and gaiety seven evenings a week, the joy would rub off, but he played the role of miserable son of a bitch well. Never did let the bottom of your cup show, though.

"I'll take a little more," said Harden. "Thanks Emmett."

I held up a hand, then went back to nursing my first drink. A tip of the whiskey bottle preceded a light splash and then Emmett disappeared to the other side of the tavern, no doubt to scowl at someone else's merriment.

When the silence returned, then grew uncomfortable, I pushed my glass back and forth across the rough countertop. The swishing liquid inside acted as a prelude to the next exchange.

"Said something about a cavern before he died. Know anything about caves around here?"

"Well, I imagine there's plenty of caves in the area, you wander a bit away from the town. Up in the Blackjacks, maybe. Can't say I ever had occasion to explore them myself. Rory—"

"How many?"

"More than a single man could explore by his lonesome, hoss." He paused and I allowed him the slack to phrase the next thing just right. "You sure he wasn't just spittin' nonsense?"

I laughed. Could tell it didn't sound forced, more like it had escaped from the depths and didn't belong up on the surface. Harden furrowed his eyebrows, more concerned than put at ease. "Of course I'm not sure, John. It's just . . ." I pushed the glass back and forth between my hands again; the moisture along the bar eased the scraping sound, but didn't stop it from occupying my attention. I paused, unsure if I really wanted to launch into this story. I met Harden's eyes and they assured me they were sober enough. I wasn't wasting my time.

Letting out an overdramatic sigh in place of a prologue, I went on. "Henry Taff."

"God rest his soul," put in the sheriff.

I raised my drink in answer. "Henry was my daddy's best friend, so the day that bloodsoaked train pulled into the station, he and Wilhelmina took me in. Didn't even think twice about it, even when the rest of the people gathered there wouldn't look at me. Never mind that the Taffs didn't have the means to do so, and had no guarantee of any of my parents' money. They saw it was the Christian thing to do, and didn't look back. Only other person who showed a speck of kindness was the sheriff."

"Sounds like a good man. Handsome, too."

I continued, unable to suppress a smirk. "Anyway, their house took a little getting used to, situated on the outskirts of Buzzard's Edge as it was, but they filled it with love all the same."

Harden hadn't taken a drink throughout the entire beginning of the story, as if determined to award his full attention. I appreciated that.

"All I have is a gut feeling, but I suspect the Taffs always wanted a kid, and even though the circumstances weren't what they hoped for, they had one from there on out. 'You're welcome here as long as you need us, Rory.' Willie repeated that like a mantra. Tucked me into a spare bed in a room no bigger than a closet. I didn't always sleep well, though."

"How could you?" said Harden softly. "After what you seen aboard that train?"

"That was part of it," I said, looking straight ahead at the filthy mirror hung over the top-shelf liquor. Even if the mirror's angle was right, I wouldn't have been able to make out my own reflection through the mire. As I weighed the next sentence, a fly buzzed by my ear and landed on the mirror, making itself at home in the grime. That was alright. Fit right in there. "Mostly, I expected he'd come back for me."

"Noose."

I nodded. "And truth be told, I kind of wanted him to. I'd lay in bed every night listening to the sounds outside my window. Every footstep, I wanted it to be him so bad, I convinced myself it would be. Nine times out of ten, it was some drunk farmer wandering back from Lynch's. The tenth was my imagination. Nothing outside my window. Even so, I thought he must be hiding, waiting for his time to strike and finish what he started. He gave me a bullet that day, you know."

Harden nodded his head. I'd told him before, showed it to him. Probably upwards of twenty times, but he didn't want to be impolite.

"I'd squeeze that bullet in my little fist while I tried to go to sleep, and if that vicious, evil smile cropped up in my window, I'd have used it. Don't know how. I guess I didn't ever really think that far ahead. Damnable thing is, he told me I'd be delivering a message, and I don't even know what it was. Not that it mattered, because nobody wanted to listen anyway. Guess I failed, John."

"How long that go on?"

"Years," I answered. "By night, I'd do all that. Sometimes even hum that old shoo fly song. You know the one?"

Harden whistled a bar in response.

"Yeah." I laughed, a little more life in it this time. "That's the one. Same goddamn song he sang the first time I saw him. Thought maybe I could summon him or something. But he never showed. I kept my ear to the ground for him; that's how I learned all about the crew of miscreants he'd used before— his gang, if you will—Crane being one of them. But Noose Holcomb and the other four? Seemed they went to ground the moment he departed that train. The name inspired fear, but nobody heard so much as a fart from them."

"Until last week," finished Harden.

"Until last week." I sipped my drink, not loving the way the alcohol sat in my stomach, but I'd chatted my way to a bad case of dry mouth. "Word is every one of those fuckers brought something to the crew. Noose was their leader, of course. Simon Crane was the scientist, the brains. Needed dynamite to pull off a job, they relied on him to cook that treacherous shit up."

Harden shifted uncomfortably in his seat. "Rory, where are you going with this?"

I continued, refusing to be derailed. "Dorrance. That's the big motherfucker you want to watch out for. We're talkin' circus strong, impossibly strong. If half the stories I dug up about that big bastard are true, shit, I'm not lookin' forward to catching up with him. Edwards is Noose's right-hand man. Supposedly you don't get to the boss unless you can justify your intentions to Edwards's satisfaction. Supposed to be pretty good with a knife, but I don't know what else he brings to the table, and that honestly worries me."

"Oh, that all?"

"Oh no, my friend, that's just the top of the cactus. We haven't even gotten to the roots yet. When that guard on the train shot Noose, the bullet just bounced off. Didn't miss. Bounced off."

"Been through this, Rory. I'm not saying you don't remember it that way, but last I checked, ain't no bulletproof men out there."

I stared down at my drink, but decided against another sip. "I bet that yesterday, if somebody told you what would happen to those people at the bank, you'd declare it impossible." I let the accusation hang there, knowing Harden wouldn't answer it. "Bulletproof men aside, the whole damn town watched him dangle from the gallows and laugh about it 'til they cut him down. They hung him high and he refused to die. Or is that me misremembering again?"

"Nope. Don't s'pose it is." He sulked.

"Last member of that crew is a woman. I've heard her called by a few names, but the most common seems to be Merella. There's plenty of men that can't report on her 'cause they set out to learn more and never came back. The ones that did return were dismissed as lunatics, an easy enough notion to agree with if it's one or two, but not when it's upwards of ten. This Merella did something to their minds. I suspect she also keeps Holcomb from harm."

"A witch?"

"I wouldn't argue with that label."

Satisfied with his whiskey for the moment, Harden dug in his pocket and retrieved a hand-rolled cigarette leaking tobacco. Speaking out the side of his mouth as he lit it, he said, "Gotta tell you, hoss, I don't put much stock in magic or hoodoo or whatever."

"I suggest you open your mind a bit, John. All kinds of shit in this world science can't touch with a ten-foot pole. Nor does it want to."

Harden nodded, the flared cigarette tip leaving orange tracers and providing the only answer I expected. A few smoky inhales and exhales accompanied the ambience of the tavern. When the silence had eaten up enough of the night to replace an appropriate segue, Harden changed the subject.

"So what's next?"

"You ever had ants in your house, John?"

He jerked his head away like he might be close enough to catch some crazy, narrow eyes completing the picture. "It's fuckin' Arizona, kid. Who the fuck ain't had ants in their house at some point?"

"Yeah, me too. We used to get 'em in the spring when I was little. I swear, every year I'd spot the first one, always alone. A scout, maybe. Henry Taff would turn all red in the face, not really mad, mind you, but like something told him that year would be different and we wouldn't have to deal with an infestation. Got to be I looked forward to sharing that first sighting because Willie'd laugh at him and that would get me laughing, which would break his pissy facade down. He'd mash the wily little fucker with his boot and every year impart the same wisdom."

I moved the glass back and forth, making like I was trying to remember the wording just so, but it stuck with me like so many of his sayings, I could've recited the litany in my sleep. "Used to say, 'No pest fixin' to stir up a shitstorm ever travels alone.' He'd follow that up by saying that particular creepy crawler got caught first, but its brethren would be upon us in no time. Perhaps searching for vengeance, perhaps opportunity."

John smirked. Not meaning to make fun, but with a trace of mockery all the same. The kind of grin that would earn a stranger a meal consisting of his own teeth. "Didn't bother you he was talkin' about bugs?"

"Was he? Henry Taff was just about the smartest and most decent man I ever knew. Not to speak ill of my daddy, just happened I got to know Henry for longer. Maybe he meant ants, and maybe he meant the way of this world. Either way, now that Crane's shown his face, I'm gonna be listenin' even harder for those names. Kinda hoped you might do the same. Pass any pertinent information my way."

I stood and fished out a handful of change to cover my drink. It clinked on the countertop, coming to rest in a puddle of condensation and excess booze. Harden held up a hand to signal Lynch, ordering another drink instead of closing the tab. As I laid my hand on his thick, meaty shoulder, he murmured, "Dorrance, Edwards, and Merella. That the size of it?"

"Don't forget Holcomb."

Harden nodded like some great deity had control of his head on a string. It was still bobbing when I walked out the door.

CHAPTER 4

GHOST STORIES

It took about five minutes to walk from Lynch's Tavern back home to Wilhelmina Taff and the ranch. I hadn't drunk much, but walked slowly anyway to sober up and let the sharp aroma dissipate. She wouldn't say anything if I came in the door in my suds, but she would hit me with a very disappointed, very motherly look.

I focused on kicking pebbles and little clusters of sand, sending them skittering across the dry ground with a soft scratching sound. Before long, the subtle outline of the farmhouse I called home appeared under the moon's gentle glow.

Growing up on Henry Taff's ranch meant training as a farmhand, like it or lump it. Henry and Willie—calling her ma'am never quite took—didn't start working me the first day or anything like that. Just once I settled in and became part of the family. The kind of reasonable chores thrust on every kid, big and small, to start, and then some heavier lifting to help the Taffs keep up with orders once the years started catching up with them.

I often thought about who I'd have become if the Daggett family had skipped that bloody train ride. Dad routinely delegated the jobs I now performed at sunrise to the hired help. He never said they were beneath him—at least not that I can remember—but the implication stuck out clear as day.

Henry Taff, my adoptive father, taught me everything I understood parents should teach their children. I loved him, and the word 'adoptive' sometimes slipped so far to the back of my mind, I couldn't remember any other way of life.

As I approached the house, lost in thought, the hearth's warm glow acted as an enticing beacon, standing out against the surrounding darkness. I thought of how the three of us gathered around it on cold nights, and Henry'd tell ghost stories—ones his mother had told him in front of that same hearth.

Henry had been gone five years, taken by the Lord when his heart gave out. I beat the sun out to the barn one morning with milking the cows on my mind. The atmosphere didn't sit right. Too heavy, like a giant bracing down on my shoulders. It was a rare day when I arrived outside before Henry. I recall leaving the bucket underneath a half-milked holstein and wandering back to the house, already knowing what I would find.

Something told me to run—that's what a normal person would do—but my legs carried me of their own accord. The familiar landscape of the house passed in a dreamlike state. In through the kitchen and down the hall, I trailed my fingers along the rough wooden walls. I almost hoped for a splinter to catch hold of my hand and bite into it, because after abandoning the poor dairy cow, I'd gone numb. Willie's muffled sobbing floated out into the hall and drew me in with somber tendrils. There I found her, still dressed in bedclothes, laid across the body of her husband, begging for any god who would listen to take this cruel joke back.

Even the thud of my ass hitting the floor as my legs gave out didn't pull Willie from her grief. I expected hot tears to cascade down my cheeks, the same old feeling after Noose abandoned the train car and left me among the rotting carrion, but they refused to fall.

I hadn't even seen two decades, yet I had known the loss of two fathers. I loved Henry dearly, but as tormented as my heart felt, it didn't hold a candle to the weight that crushed Willie. Slumped to the floor in a useless heap, I made a silent promise to myself that I would never leave her alone. She'd done me a kindness once a long time ago, and arguably every day since. I aimed to take care of her as long as she'd have me.

Now, with the scent of whiskey lost to the desert wind, I went inside. Willie sat by the hearth, busying herself with crochet. A quick glance up and a half-smile acknowledged my arrival. She'd waited up for me. Probably heard all kinds of rumors about the showdown with Crane, but rather than peppering me with questions, we enjoyed a comfortable silence.

After a while, I broke it.

"I was thinking about him on the walk home. How he used to tell us stories right by that fire."

A giggle escaped. "Henry and his ghost stories. He was incorrigible, I'll give him that. You'd go to bed, Rory, and I'd tell him those terrible yarns would keep you up all night."

"I sleep better nowadays."

"I'm glad," she said, and we resumed our silence, accompanied only by the crackling fire.

We buried Henry on a Tuesday. I remember it rained. It almost never rained in Buzzard's Edge, but it did that day. Mr. Meyer, the proprietor of the town's cooperage, moonlighted crafting the odd pinebox when one of the residents required it. Make no mistake, anyone who stopped drawing breath received a casket, but those who could pay, those who lived a bit closer to the center of town, were lowered into the ground in style.

We laid Henry to rest in one of the nicest coffins I'd ever seen, keeping in mind I'd witnessed the construction of more than a dozen the week the Taffs took me in. Thirteen coffins belonging to the richest people to ever grace the town's records, and not a single one furnished with the time, care, and love that went into Henry Taff's. The fact that my adoptive father garnered that kind of respect, despite living hand-to-mouth all his life made me feel something I'm not sure I could put a name to, but pride is close enough.

Rain pelted down from the sky, soaking the nicest outfit I owned. It felt appropriate somehow. A momentary reprieve from the constant heat of the Arizona sun. We took a break from our suffering to honor a man who consistently brought joy to the lives of those around him, even when faced with hardship. He couldn't win, but that didn't stop him trying.

After committing Henry to the earth, Willie and I walked home to a house that would never feel quite full again. She held my hand, displaying a strength I wouldn't have thought her capable of that day. Still, every time I looked at her, she appeared ready to collapse. We didn't say a word on the way home. Didn't have to. It'd be a cold day in hell before we abandoned each other.

Weeks passed following Crane's death, his scientific endeavors locked away in that safe at the sheriff's office. I didn't ask, but Harden had suggested, during one of his check-in visits, that the safe wound up in an unused storage closet because no one who made use of that building felt comfortable around it. Harden had the same problem I faced in the desert; a bit of a damned if you do, damned if you don't predicament. Eventually, they forgot about the safe's contents and the nerves died down. Business returned to usual. Not just around the sheriff's office, but everywhere in Buzzard's Edge, even on Taff Ranch.

That's where I was when they came for me.

Damn smart move for a couple reasons. Mid-afternoon with the work mostly done, I didn't even have a shirt on, never mind anything deadlier than a spade to defend myself with. Add to that, I had about as much energy left as a horse that just hauled a fat man up a mountain.

Dorrance came into sight first, materializing on the horizon and solidifying against an errant dust cloud. I'd heard plenty of stories about him, big as an ox and twice as goddamn mean, but I never saw an ox quite so large as this one. Decked out in boots that squeezed his feet and a constricting pair of jeans, he strode forward. He wore a shirt so massive, a normal man would need directions to get out of it, but it hugged his muscular body, cut off at the sleeves to make sure his arms received the proper attention. When he got close enough that I could see his face, his hateful eyes—the only thing small about him—assessed the land for threats before alighting on me.

Thunder rolled, an avalanche of rocks crashing down the side of a mountain as he spoke. His voice was so deep it seemed to emanate from the earth itself, channeled up through his feet before bursting forth from his mouth.

"If this the guy that gave Crane his comeuppance, he don't look like much."

The phrasing puzzled me. Dorrance studied me as though he expected an answer, his beady little eyes hovering over his bulbous, crooked nose. That's when I noticed he wasn't alone.

My brain and my eyes worked overtime to convince me the slight woman had hid behind the broad giant up until this point, but that's not what happened. Merella hadn't stood there a moment ago; I'd cross my heart and hope to die on that point. No, she appeared from a gash in the universe not ten feet away from me. Some kind of shimmering magic allowed her entry, and its glossy remnants still danced in the air a moment later. A black dress covered her, appearing both living and somehow wet. Part of me wanted to lay a hand on it and confirm the mirage, but I feared it might take a bite out of me.

"Looks can be deceiving." The words slithered to my ears, devoid of emotion, but her mouth didn't move. On this, my brain, eyes, and heart agreed.

My eyes flicked back and forth between them while also keeping watch for any more arrivals. If Edwards or Holcomb were here, they hid well. The ranch didn't offer much cover.

A grin spread across Dorrance's face, as if he'd seen something he liked. The kind of look a man got setting down before a home-cooked meal. Merella's face betrayed nothing, appearing almost bored as she stared through me.

Instead of copping to what caught his fancy, Dorrance whistled the opening melody of "Shoo Fly". This visit wasn't random. It wasn't even vengeance. It crashed down on me in an instant. Holcomb knew me, knew who I was, had probably kept tabs on me for the better part of fifteen years. Cold sweat drained from every pore as I considered my next move. Every possibility struck me as poor at best.

When Dorrance finished the verse, he maneuvered to the chorus, adding a ritardando to the end, bringing it to rest with a dramatic flourish. A countdown. When he stopped, the three of us stared at each other. Silence reigned. Even the bugs quit their chittering to avoid missing the dance.

One of Merella's bone-white hands crept from beneath the black dress, fingers wriggling like an orgy of rattlesnakes. My body went rigid like petrified wood. Even my breathing came to an abrupt halt, begging my lungs to expel the air trapped in there. The cold sweat built. Panic must have shown in my eyes, because Dorrance's grin grew with bemusement. These two appeared from the ether to watch me suffocate upon my own two feet, and there was nothing I could do. My bladder released, combatting the cold sweat with a temporary warmth, and uttering a soundless signal that enough was enough. That didn't alleviate the pressure building in my upper body, however. I begged for mercy with my eyes, but found only amusement.

"Ain't done with you by a long shot, shoo fly."

Dorrance wound back one meaty fist and let it loose like a runaway train. Unable to dodge, my head welcomed the sudden darkness.

CHAPTER 5

AMID THE CINDERS

When I came to, the tightness and burning on my bare skin didn't make sense, what with the sun dipping below the horizon. A sunburn, I guessed. It covered the top half of my body and made me grimace whenever I moved.

For better or worse, the pain distracted me from the smell lingering in the air.

Dusk hid the hanging smoke, floating up toward the sky to join a veil of clouds. I probably would have missed it if not for the acrid scent of burning. Shooting to my feet, I came face-to-face with the husk of the Taff's house—my house—engulfed in flames that reached high into the air and tickled the sky. All the effort to pull my battered body to its feet disintegrated like the flame-riddled beams and I nearly collapsed to my knees.

"Willie." Her name escaped my lips as naturally as breathing, but the fire's crackle—not unlike the hearth—stole it away.

I covered my face with one arm and plunged through a barrier of flames, not considering the addition of more burns to my repertoire of injuries. The blaze had already consumed parts of the house while I lay unconscious, thanks to the witch's magic and the brute force of Holcomb's protector. Time reduced the fire to a smolder, but the thick, noxious smoke poured from the house's carcass, choking my progress.

"Willie!" I screamed, over and over, receiving no answer. My spinning head roiled and tumbled until I could barely keep on my feet. I didn't even know which room I'd wandered into, but if I didn't get out soon, I wouldn't see the sunrise again. Coils of black smoke extended, like the arms of a demon trying to grab me and drag me back into the flaming wreckage of my home. For a moment, I considered letting them, but pushed forward instead.

For Henry.

For Willie.

For Mom and Dad.

Giving up wouldn't make them proud.

I tore my arms free from the smoke's grasp and barreled into another room, the smoke thinner here. The right direction at last, but the murky air revealed nothing. One more push through a wall of blistering heat and the moon's light washed over me. My legs discovered one last bastion of strength, enough to drag my battered body a little further from the house before calling it quits.

Underneath the radiant glow of the full moon, I had one last thought before darkness called me home for the second time that day. Maybe, just maybe, Willie had gotten away. Maybe I hadn't lost everything yet.

As it turned out, I did get to see the sun rise again. Actually, it was high in the sky by the time I came to, feeling like ten tons of baked shit scraped across the rough sandy ground. I didn't recall partaking in any activity that would have broken a rib, but something felt wrong in that vicinity. My lungs functioned at about half capacity, wheezing for a hint of breath even in the clear morning air.

I tried pulling myself to my feet, but my body replied with a hearty "fuck you" and stayed flat on the ground, the stubborn cuss. As a compromise, it allowed me to turn my head toward what remained of the ranch. Trickles of smoke climbed to the sky, a dull reflection of the horror I'd encountered last night. The black smoke had dyed everything it touched a sooty stygian black. The color of death.

Nothing moved inside the gutted remains of the house. When I could get up, I would check, but I feared I wouldn't find Willie. Not in the way I'd grown accustomed to, at least. Whether she'd burned up in the blaze, escaped with her life, or worse yet, been taken by that mismatched duo of mercenaries, I wouldn't find her puttering around making breakfast or even just watching her boys work with a contented smile. Not your average morning, in other words.

Minutes, or maybe hours—fucked if I could tell the difference—passed. Perhaps it was the sun positioning itself directly overhead to cook my ass some more that finally encouraged me to get going. I couldn't just lay there waiting for death. Every step shot anguish up to my skull, making some detours to hit my other extremities, as well. I hobbled toward the house, knowing that regardless of the result, I wouldn't like what I found.

Searching the house took an ungodly amount of time. Wood splintered under my feet, but had the decency to remain muffled so I could hear any movement. None came, but that didn't set my mind at ease. The witch and the giant said they weren't done with me, but had neglected to provide a timeline. Every corner I rounded held the potential for the charred black walls to shift, revealing the woman under the cloak. Each room I stumbled in and out of held its breath. I shook my head, thinking Merella and Dorrance had every opportunity to kill me where I stood and hadn't. Just like Noose all those years ago.

Something in this universe wanted to ensure I suffered properly. Or someone, at least.

Each room seemed emptier than the last. Deep down I knew that empty meant empty. Doesn't make sense for one thing devoid of matter to be more devoid than the last, but I know what I felt. It wasn't something I could quantify, more like hope disappearing a little further into the distance every time I walked into a room where I'd spent my teenage years, still unable to account for my adoptive mom.

My bedroom was the hardest place to enter. So familiar for so long, I hardly recognized it, reduced to rubble as it was. I grimaced, allowing my eyes to mourn the loss of comfort, of belonging. Amid the cinders, a small patch of chrome glinted in the sunlight that poked through the ruined roof. The remnants of my bed half covered my revolver, my last piece of Henry. Save the part reflecting the sunlight, the rest appeared smoggy and charred, but not deformed. Assuming it might be salvageable, I tucked it into the back of my pants, only realizing after I'd done it that the barrel might have retained enough heat to solder my asscrack shut. Thankfully, time had cooled it. I went to leave, when another gleam caught my eye. An item that didn't want to be forgotten, sending up a distress signal before I could abandon it to its blackened grave.

I knew what it was even as my fingers closed around it, feeling its warmth. Rather than leftover embers, the warmth came from life, from a promise. The bullet. The very one Noose had pressed into my hand the last time we met. Too fortuitous to be circumstance. I tucked the bullet into a pocket and gave it a pat to ensure its safety before continuing.

Finally, I came to the last room and found it every bit as abandoned as the others. Something was different in this one, however. Nothing my eyes could pick up on, but a hint of an odor. Scorched meat. My heart sank and my stomach jumped, passing each other on their respective journeys. Understanding the origin of the smell, I gagged. Probably would have vomited anything in my stomach, except for a tinge of sweetness that soothed my gut and my nerves.

I might have missed her if I hadn't checked closely. The fire had reduced her to bone shards and teeth, half-hidden beneath the debris. My eyes didn't recognize her remains, but my heart did.

I wished Dorrance had taken her. Or the witch. Maybe put her under the same forsaken spell she laid on me, leaving Willie unable to move a muscle while they dragged her back to Noose. At least then there'd be the possibility of seeing her again. I wasn't ready. I wanted to cry, but the tears wouldn't come—burned and dried out like everything else around here. So instead, I screamed. Screamed until the inside of my throat stung as raw and red as the rest of my body.

I only stopped when my throat refused to relinquish any more sound.

Caverns was the only thing I had to go on. Possibly the ramblings of a man in the midst of losing his mind, but maybe a man who didn't know any better divulging a hidden truth. I couldn't think straight. Between the loss of Willie, the sun poisoning, the knock to the head, and what might be the lingering effects of Merella's spell, I was a fucking mess, to put it lightly.

I needed a place to recuperate for a few days, but only one location came to mind, and it was a bad idea.

CHAPTER 6

WELCOME HOME

Before I left, I gathered what the fire had left of Wilhelmina and committed her to one of her favorite vases, the one she always kept chuparosa in. It was cornflower blue, and whenever she gathered the pale red flowers, I always remarked on how nice the colors matched. Brought a smile to her face every time. I'd attended enough funerals in my life to know the proper things to say when returning one of God's children to the earth, but none of that seemed appropriate here, so I shared some favorite memories, as much positivity as I could muster, and a few things that will stay between me, Willie, and any intelligent creators who may have eavesdropped.

I fought the urge to think anything positive of my attackers, but a cautious relief washed over me when I noted their arson streak hadn't extended to the barn. I held my breath walking into the stable, sure that a menagerie of murdered animals waited behind the door: slit throats and headshots. I clenched my teeth and squeezed my eyes shut as the door creaked open. Ghost nickered in greeting, her black-and-white spots a welcome sight for sore eyes. The other livestock lowed in serendipitous celebration and I couldn't keep a smile from my face. The last twelve hours had taken a lot from me, but not everything.

Listening carefully for any stray sounds—the kind belonging to boots rather than hooves—I overfed them all. A task which usually took less than five minutes stretched to twenty, then half an hour, with my diminished capacity. Promising the scared animals I'd come back, I mounted Ghost and departed Taff Ranch, pointed toward the center of Buzzard's Edge.

Ghost trotted slowly and my sore ass thanked her for that. The leisurely trip allowed me to take in the surroundings as the spread out farmhouses gave way to stores and other businesses. I didn't visit this part of town any more often than necessary. Too close to my former life. As the businesses gave way to homes, more densely packed and garish the farther I went along, I felt a pull. Almost magnetic in a way, like I was being drawn toward a moment I'd avoided for too long.

I passed homes so extravagant they appeared embarrassed by the mud-riddled streets which had the audacity to exist before their bold facades. The shamelessness of it all nearly brought me to laughter, but I couldn't quite summon it. Sadness brimmed too near the surface, knowing my destination.

Though Ghost and I took our time, our arrival was inevitable. I couldn't fathom how one might reach a high enough altitude to look down on Buzzard's Edge, but if such a method existed, I'd wager you could find Daggett Manor at the exact center of it all. The houses that seemed outlandish at first glance paled in comparison to my family's two-story residence, and despite not laying eyes on it for fifteen years, the place dragged me back to my eight-year-old state of mind.

Daddy kept a hitching post out front for guests, and although my last name begged to differ, that's exactly what I felt like. I tied Ghost up, mindlessly utilizing the type of knot employed in front of the tavern. Probably wasn't necessary out here. Ghost was a workhorse and I pitied the thief that tried to make off with her. I scoped out the neighborhood before starting up the walk, perhaps more out of paranoia than curiosity. The packed-together houses we'd passed not ten minutes before were a distant memory compared to the privacy afforded by the street in front of Daggett Manor. I could see the other houses, but I'd have to come outside and pace for half a minute to meet another living soul.

Time hadn't treated the place well, and I suspected I might be its first visitor since we closed the front door to hop on that ill-fated train. As I approached the door, Ghost called from the street. It sounded like a warning, but I was admittedly nervous and might be putting words in the horse's mouth. Nonetheless, I hesitated. The street remained empty. Any remaining neighbors displayed the decency of staying inside and leaving me to this hideous business.

The door creaked as it swung open, fighting against rusty hinges. I'd tried the knob in a moment of optimism, but when it actually turned, my stomach inched upward, coming to rest at the base of my throat. Concerned that my parents' house might be sheltering an unwanted resident or two, I drew the charred gun from the back of my pants. I hadn't tested it, but if it refused to fire, it would at least crack a skull.

I entered, revolver first. No trace of urine or filth to suggest a down-on-their-luck outer edge citizen had broken in to escape the harsh sun. I don't know what I expected Dorrance might smell like, but I didn't lend much credence to a man that size existing without some kind of rancid musk to give him away. The witch wouldn't give off a scent, though. I couldn't be sure of that, of course, but the fact that she could appear from thin air put some sense behind it.

The one smell that did make itself known was mildew, telling the story of time past. Some god-fearing neighbor had entered the house over the years. The boarded up windows that choked off the outside light made that clear enough. I made my way to a window and tried to tear some boards away, but they hadn't given way to rot yet and the nails held fast. I'd need some tool

I didn't currently possess to make this look more like a home and less like a cave.

Cave. Cavern.

No, too easy. I continued on.

A creak accompanied every step, announcing my arrival. Even though I'd left the front door open, the amount of afternoon sunlight that entered left a lot to be desired. The echo of my footsteps created the illusion of company; intrepid explorers blazing a trail through this uncharted wilderness. I cursed myself for not having the foresight to bring something to illuminate the way, although I think the sight of flames dancing across the wall, even contained to the head of a match, would have sent me running.

"Shoo fly . . ."

A whispered voice stopped me in my tracks. It didn't boast the thunderous resonance of Dorrance or the arrogance of Holcomb. It was higher-pitched; more childlike.

". . . don't bother me." Laughter followed. Not cruel, but serving as an epilogue to a fabulous joke its owner had told. The smack of hands clapping together came next, startling me. "I have no wings, but still can fly. Have no eyes, but sometimes cry. What, pray tell, oh what am I?"

A hush settled over the house as a rapid what the fuck? raced through my mind. The answer was who, not what.

Nathan Edwards.

Crane, Dorrance, and Merella played their roles within Holcomb's gang, though Edwards's purpose was less clear. A court jester, perhaps. The stories I'd dug up on him all said the same. The assault began with words, riddles, but turned violent when the victim's answer well ran dry. A jester he might be, but those same tales told of Edwards's considerable skill with a blade.

"Not even a guess? How disappointing."

"Wait!" I said, trying to forestall the stabbing. The echoes of our voices bounced around the desolate house, making it no clearer where he might be located. "Give me a minute to think."

I took his silence as acquiescence, and I did think, but not about the riddle. The light was too dim to show much of the room's layout. I had to rely on memory. I closed my eyes and tried to picture eight-year-old Rory returning from playing outside, bursting through the door and into the foyer. Forward and to the right lay the sitting room, leading to Mom and Dad's bedroom. No admittance for Rory that way, but enough open space for an assassin-in-waiting. Straight ahead was the dining room. Some afternoons, I glimpsed the table being set by Mrs. Carlisle, but I didn't even think about going in there until I washed up. To the left sat the parlor, not all that different from the sitting room, if I'm honest. Another stuffy room filled with furniture you couldn't play on, giving Edwards plenty of space to hide.

Stuffy. Puffy. Cloud. What can fly without wings, cries without eyes?

"A cloud." The answer flew out before I could give it a second pass to be sure it made sense, half mumbled under my breath.

"Well played, sir. An easy one, to be sure. A sporting chance to herald the beginning of our game."

I didn't like this fucker.

He had to be in one of those three rooms. Past the sitting room in the master bedroom was too far from the entrance and the way his voice carried, he sounded like he was all around me. Between the dining room and parlor, a staircase climbed to the second floor, hiding the kitchen and servant quarters. Too far to be heard clearly.

"Something more challenging this time, I think." His voice came from the same level as me. Most likely he traveled as he spoke, mimicking a mouse with his footsteps to avoid detection.

The next riddle originated from a new location.

"When I eat, I live. When I breathe, I live. When I drink, I die. What am I?"

The answer came to me immediately—how could it not?—but I held it close to buy time. Straight ahead or a little to the left. His voice didn't come from the parlor, which left two choices. To buy time, and cover my movement, I repeated his riddle back to him. I could hear the smug smile in his response.

"A challenge, yes, but surely not too difficult for the likes of Rory Daggett. My friends think so highly of you, boy."

"Do they now? Why's that?" I edged closer, but still couldn't tell. It was almost as though he was standing at the nexus of the two rooms.

Edwards clucked his tongue in response. "A riddle exists between us, good sir. And until it is solved, I'm afraid we cannot move to other areas of conversation."

"Fire, then."

"Why, Mr. Daggett, I believe you've been holding out on me. That answer positively flew from the tip of your tongue. Nonetheless, you are correct. Fire grows as it consumes. It flourishes as it draws the oxygen from the very air that surrounds us. Sometimes from the lungs of its victims. A terrible way to go, to be sure. Don't you think?" He allowed the statement to hang, expecting a rise from me, and his shrill voice nearly drew one, but I kept control. With a hint of disappointment, he continued. "But drink, that is what the flame truly fears. Sometimes that takes the shape of a liquid, although it can mean time, as well. A blaze extinguished by a decided lack of resources. Don't you find that to be true?"

His voice grated, wheedling under my skin. Edwards didn't disguise the self-importance in his tone. He didn't just think he was smarter than me—although, he did think that, true enough. Nathan Edwards thought he was the smartest motherfucker in the whole damn state of Arizona. But that was alright. The longer he talked, the more I zeroed in on his position.

"Maybe I am holding out on you. Maybe it just . . . flickered to my mind."

"Marvelous," he said. "A man with jokes. I do love a good joke. Mr. Daggett, as much as I'd love to while away the afternoon with you, I must be going soon. Though I did hope you'd entertain one more question."

"Certainly," I said through gritted teeth, though I only half-listened. My eyes closed once more.

"Very well. Perhaps something a bit more plainspoken this time around. For a man of the people such as yourself." He paused, allowing the atmosphere to develop for his final delivery.

"Why did Beethoven not complete his Unfinished Symphony?"

I grinned, knowing he couldn't see me in the darkness of the oversized foyer. His voice carried as if it came from the dining room and the sitting room at once, but that's because it came from the wall between the two. Not a week went by in the early 1870s where little Rory Daggett didn't have his britches hauled down and his ass paddled, once in a while by Dad, but more often by one of the male servants. The reason? I'd come in from playing, and instead of heading upstairs to my room, I would hide. Not behind any of that expensive furniture or anything like that, though.

No, my hiding spot of choice was the dumbwaiter installed between the two rooms I suspected Edwards of spying on me from. My parents hated its existence. Didn't ask for it during the construction of the house and blocked it with an end table when the workers explained it couldn't be removed. With the lack of light, I couldn't be certain, but everything pointed to Edwards being in there, door cracked and waiting for me to happen by, so he could stick me once he'd finished his game. I wouldn't disappoint him.

"You're awfully quiet, Mr. Daggett." The smile had retreated from his voice. "Dare I ask if I've stumped you?"

Too close to his hiding spot to answer him, I moved quickly. If my luck held, maybe I'd avoid barking a shin against the end table. My fingers brushed the sitting room doorframe, careful not to make a sound. Out of options, I relied on outdated muscle memory and grabbed at where I knew the small door to be.

My fingers closed on fabric and I yanked him from his hidey-hole. My hidey-hole. I'd gotten the drop on him, but the little fucker was lightning-quick with those knives, just like the stories said. A couple of metal snikt sounds rang out as pain bloomed on my forearm. Hot lashes preceded a wetness dripping down my arms. So many cuts for such a short period of time. Each one stung in agony.

Refusing to relinquish my hold on him, I wrenched him from the dumbwaiter and smashed his small body into the wall. Breath whooshed from his lungs. It was the longest he'd gone without talking since his first words crept out of the dark.

"Where is he?" The ragged tone of my voice surprised me. Goddamn I needed some rest after the last twenty-four hours.

"A riddle. Exists. Between us." The same mantra as before, but with my bleeding forearm shoved into his throat, he struggled to give up that much.

A sharp pain erupted in my side, followed once again by swishing metal, as though his hands moved faster than sound. I lifted the man by his collar once more, raised him over my head and slammed him to the floor. A series of clangs proclaimed the freedom of the knives—at least two of them—

but I didn't dare assume that was all he had on him. Alternating between left and right hooks, I felt more cuts open, flesh tearing on my knuckles. It was comforting to know that even though some of the blood flowing belonged to me, most of it was his.

A little voice inside told me he'd had enough, so I threw a few more jabs and then listened to the telltale signs of lingering life; raspy breathing with a whistling accompaniment and a groaning sound I don't believe Edwards knew he was making.

"Beethoven didn't complete the Unfinished Symphony because it was Schubert who wrote it. Don't test a rich kid, Mr. Edwards."

His wheeze increased, an attempt at laughter that didn't quite resemble the desired product.

"Right you are, Mr. Daggett." A hacking cough served as an interlude between sentences. "Seems you've bested me in our game of wits."

"Wits, sure."

"There's a book . . . of matches in my vest pocket . . . Mr. Daggett. I wonder . . . if you'd allow me some light to choke to death by."

I didn't move. Incapacitated as he was, I didn't trust this trickster. Nonetheless, I had two sets of parents that both raised me better than to deny a dying man his final wish.

"When you climbed into that dumbwaiter, you had to move the table, right?"

Edwards gurgled in the affirmative.

"Still some candles on there?"

"You know . . . I believe there were." Some people just had to spit out six words where one would do, even when bleeding into their lungs.

I reached cautiously for his chest, feeling the matches through his shirt. One truth, at least. I drew them out. Edwards, coiled as a spring, made no move to reach for any hidden blades. With the matches retrieved, I put a boot on his chest and stood, taking care to put a little more weight than necessary on his ribcage. He didn't scream, but an uncomfortable whimper escaped his lips. The table stood where I expected it'd be, candles scattered across the top as promised.

I struck a match, allowing its light to reach Edwards before touching it to the wick. Fast as he was, the gleam of the knife under the fire's watchful eye betrayed him. He plunged the blade into the top of my boot, straight down through the foot, and possibly into his own belly. The agony in my foot rivaled the heat displayed in my hand, but my subconscious reached for the revolver tucked away in my pants before he could withdraw the buried knife and search out a second destination for it.

A deafening bang and a display of light that put the single match to shame filled the room. It provided a momentary glimpse of Edwards's head bursting, releasing the riddles no one had ever heard, nor ever would.

I struck another match and lit the candles, hoping the scent might cover the emerging odor of shit and blood. I would've killed for the smell of must all of the sudden. Taking care not to look at the mess I'd made, I rounded the corner into the sitting room, plopped to the floor, and hung my head. The exhaustion of the last twenty-four hours had caught up with me, and even if Noose Holcomb himself entered my childhood home, I couldn't have summoned the energy to draw on him.

Four members of Holcomb's gang met, two dead, and I stood no closer to surmising his plans or his hiding place. One thing was clear: too many coincidences lately.

CHAPTER 7

HIDE AND SEEK

Winding down didn't come easy. With so many shifty characters showing up in my life lately, it felt like the next impending visit hung over my head. I'd endured three such appointments so far and hoped that, like Mr. Dickens's A Christmas Carol, they'd done it all in one night. The sentiment might have held a little more water if two of them weren't still out there drawing breath. I could worry myself ragged, but I needed rest and time to think. Both could be done here, but a few tweaks might make the place more bearable.

First order of business was bandaging those knife wounds. Most of the scratches on my arms were superficial. As little as I wanted to dabble with any more fire, a little hot oil and some of those matches cauterized them nicely. I'm only glad no one was around to hear me squeal. The foot wound required some pressure dressing after the bleeding stopped. The sitting room overflowed with useless linen and I didn't figure anybody would mind if I borrowed some to prevent having to amputate my foot.

With my body back in working order, I set to cleaning up the foyer. For Christ's sake, I didn't even shut the door right away. Any uppity neighbor that happened by would've found themselves treated to a front row seat of the half-painted entryway. If anyone saw, I just hoped they would write it off to the new tenant using a particularly dark and grotesque shade of red not to their taste.

As much as I knew it would've given my mother a coronary, I led Ghost indoors before shutting and locking the door. I stationed her right inside the sitting room while I hauled Edward's remains to the back garden. More fodder for nosy neighbors. This young upstart just moved in and he's painting the walls and digging up the garden before he even gets around to dusting the window sills.

Truth be told, I didn't see any neighbors. Just knew from experience they were keeping an eye out from down the road. Before that fateful train ride, I couldn't get into anything resembling trouble without some snitchy old woman tattling to Mom and Dad about it, most times before I even arrived at home. Hell, that's half the reason I hid in the fuckin' dumbwaiter all those years. Point was, I'd have to be careful.

With the remains of Edwards disposed of, I barricaded the front door and joined Ghost in the sitting room. A lady of refined manners, she'd avoided shitting on the floor so far, though I'd do well to bring her out back when energy allowed. I collapsed on one of the couches, smearing gore and grime all over it; a childhood revenge achieved that I couldn't give a damn less about.

"Don't look at me like that," I said to the horse as I pulled my hat down over my face. I'm just gon' rest my eyes for a few minutes."

We both knew it was a lie. A single thought had time to flit through my mind before sleep wrapped me in its welcoming embrace.

I probably should've checked the rest of the house before I sat down.

It took a minute to figure out where I was when I woke up, but upon nailing that down, the first thought that sprang to mind was the severe dry mouth plaguing me. Several other problems of various import existed, but that one took precedence. It wasn't 'I'd better grab a drink' dry, but like somebody ripped out my tongue and left it in the middle of the road to get stepped on and shit on by every passing horse. I swear I could have used it to take the paint off a barn.

Every inch of me ached, none more than my throbbing head, but on the plus side, I no longer felt a dizzying exhaustion. Also, nobody had murdered me in my sleep, so that was alright.

The house remained dark as night thanks to the makeshift shutters, so I couldn't even guess how long I'd slept. I'd find out though, because if I didn't tap the backyard well soon, a rattlesnake might take up residence in my mouth, mistaking it for the arid desert. I only hoped the well still worked.

The bright sunlight forced my eyes to a squint after I unburdened the back door and stepped outside. The great glowing orb loomed overhead, a few hours past noon. I had time. What I didn't have was any coherent memory of when I'd arrived. Since nothing woke me up except maybe Ghost flicking her tail, I assumed it'd been a competent sleep and my body felt as rested up as it was bound to get.

Sending a prayer to Poseidon and hoping he'd hear it this far inland, I gave the pump a go. A couple of scary seconds passed where the faucet relinquished nothing but dust and stale air, but soon water flowed, the nectar of the gods. I swear to sweet Jesus, that clear liquid had never tasted as good as it did right then. I drank until my stomach swelled. Satiated, the next problem kicked in as the sun started to scorch my skin again.

I retreated inside, away from the scalding heat of midday, intent on figuring out what came next. The answer came quickly.

Upstairs.

My parents built the house before I was born, one of the first and only two-story houses in all of Buzzard's Edge. I never asked why they added the second floor—seemed like I might catch a palm upside the head for impertinence—but it remained unused for a long time, until I came along. Even so long as I resided in a little crib, then a slightly bigger bed, nestled away in the corner of my parents' bedroom, no one ever went up there. I guess I don't actually know that for sure, but as far back as I can remember, the three rooms at the top of the stairs stood empty and teeming with cobwebs.

Daddy found me up there every so often. There didn't seem to be anything to get into, but I don't suppose he and Momma loved the ghostly pitter-patter of feet tapping above their heads. Like clockwork, he'd drag me down the stairs, telling me to stay where Momma could watch me. Until he didn't.

Hearing him clomp up the stairs one day, I played my role, pitching myself into a shadowy corner so he'd have to look for me. He spotted me right away, but pretended not to as per our unwritten hide and seek rules. A few moments passed and he half-heartedly searched the small upstairs before acting shocked when he discovered me. Instead of leading me downstairs, Daddy sat on the floor across from me and looked me in the eye.

"Seems you're just about old enough to be sleeping in your own room, Rory."

It wasn't a question, but I answered it anyway, opening my eyes as big as I could and nodding so fast I got dizzy.

"Do you have a favorite up here?"

Despite the explosive excitement I felt inside, I tried to stay calm. Like he said, I was old enough to earn myself an upstairs room, some privacy to do . . . whatever I wanted. The moment felt important, and I beamed as I answered him.

"I kinda like this one, actually." I leaned in and lowered my voice to a conspiratorial whisper. "It's the biggest of 'em all." Daddy nodded, visibly fighting to keep a smile from intruding upon his face. Worse still, stifling a laugh. I don't think my young pride could've withstood being made the butt of a joke. As was his custom, he faced the situation with a rare breed of stoicism.

"I reckon two strong men such as ourselves could get your bed up the stairs no problem," he said, "but there's a couple things we ought to consider."

I gestured with my hand for him to continue, a movement I'd seen him employ when one of his friends droned on a bit too long. This time the smile flickered through his thick mustache. He ran a hand down his face to try and hide it, but didn't move fast enough. By then, I no longer cared.

"Well," he said, holding up an index finger. "We'll not get too far into our plan without permission from the foreman."

I ruffled my brow at the unfamiliar word. "Foreman?"

"The boss," he said, no longer employing his hand to cover the smile.

"Momma."

"Oh yes. Without her say-so, all our planning is for naught."

I nodded. "What else?"

"We'll have to get you some more furniture to make this place look a little more like home, but it won't happen today, so I'll beg your patience. That okay?"

"From Mr. Meyer."

"Of course, only the best. And one final item on the agenda, Rory." I left him room to speak, but he shifted uncomfortably as he did so. "Will you be alright to sleep up here alone tonight?"

Shit. I hadn't thought of that. The place was all well and good with daylight streaming in the windows and fighting back the shadows, but night would tell a different tale. I didn't answer right away, trying to summon a tone more confident than I actually felt to inject into my voice. I don't know if I pulled it off, but he accepted my yes with a solemn nod, then hoisted himself to his feet, grunting like old men tend to do.

"We still don't have that permission we need, kiddo, but I think I might be able to sweet talk her. Let's go find out."

He reached for my hand as we neared the stairs, then pulled back, seeming to think better of it. I was teetering on the edge of being a grown-up after all.

I imagined I could see William Daggett walking side-by-side with little Rory as I gazed up those stairs. The memory seemed so real, I even felt a breeze tickle the hair on the back of my neck when they passed by. The soft shuffle of little feet traveled across the ceiling, raining dust down into the foyer where it met the base of the stairs.

My eyes widened.

I hadn't imagined the footsteps. Noose had one more hired goon staking the place out. No way Dorrance could move about that softly. That left the witch or some unknown entity, but that was impossible. I'd dug so deep and uncovered no other allies. I drew the charred gun and pulled back the hammer with a click that shot up the stairs. A single bullet had taken out Edwards, leaving plenty more to level this intruder.

Flickering, fading, and whatever the fuck else, we'd see if Merella could dodge a bullet.

A creaking groan escaped the first step. Fuck. That one used to be trustworthy.

With stealth out the window, I focused more on what I could see than keeping silent. A roiling darkness, suggesting hundreds, if not thousands, of evil shapes lurking, confirmed someone had boarded up these windows as well. I came to a standstill every third or fourth step, listening for the recurring footsteps. Whatever made the initial sounds lay in wait, hoping I'd be foolish enough to reveal myself.

Seems I am, I thought as I approached where I thought the top of the stairs might be. When my right foot met no more resistance, I crept into the small hallway adjoining the three rooms, coming to a stop in front of where I recalled the first doorway to be. I half expected trudging forward to result in me getting hexed into the middle of next week, though probably not killed. Noose had made it clear he preferred fucking with me over straight up killing me.

Sucking in a deep breath in case it was my last, I peered around the corner, both eyes and the barrel of the gun. No witch stood awaiting my company inside the room. My nervous heart could have dealt with that. Instead it tried to scrabble up my damn throat when I laid eyes on the skeletal figure, staring out from the darkness with its gaunt eyes. Cowardice took control of my feet, but thankfully not my bladder, and I half stepped back, half stumbled away from the door's edge.

As much as I hate to embrace my yellow side, I'm real glad I was too busy running to decorate the walls with Pip's brains.

CHAPTER 8

PIP

Candlelight flickered up the stairs, not enough to be useful, but when the skeletal creature chased me into the hall the tiny allowance of light stripped the nightmare away.

The thing that gave me such a fright was only a child, naked except for a few strategically placed rags. Although it was the first word that occurred when I saw the apparition, gaunt still seemed the most appropriate. Pale skin gave the illusion of a glow. The kid appeared to have gone without sunlight and food for quite a bit of time.

When I realized they couldn't be more than seven or eight, I chastised myself for damn near shitting my pants. I don't know what movement they made that I mistook for chasing me, but the child had retreated into the bedroom since. Probably hadn't seen another human being in months, if not longer.

Holding it by the tip, I struck one of Edwards's matches and allowed the fire to breathe life into the small hallway.

When I breathe, I live.

With my brain's cogs starting to turn again, I knew plowing into the bedroom brandishing fire might scare the kid to death, so I channeled the softest, friendliest tone I ever remember using.

"My name's Rory, and I ain't here to hurt you."

The words hung in the air, unanswered.

"You look kinda hungry, friend. If you wanna come downstairs, I bet I could fix you somethin' to keep that tummy from rumblin'."

Tummy from rumblin'? Who the fuck had I become all of the sudden?

I heard the child shifting around in there, and I pictured them backed up against the wall, pushing against it like if they went hard enough, they could melt right through and become part of the house.

"Really kid, I ain't gonna hurt you. I'm gonna come in. You don't gotta hide. Alright?"

Once more, no answer, but I didn't expect one. I shook out the match, whose flame threatened to lick my fingers, and struck a new one before slowly rounding the corner. The child—a girl, I guessed by her face—sat against the wall, arms wrapped around her knees as she stared at the floor. Wrapped in a blanket now, she appeared to rock slightly, but maybe that was just the flickering light. A quick inventory of the room showed my bed still in its place, untouched and unslept in since 1872. She hadn't opted to hide under it or even close herself in the closet. Maybe that came down to paralyzing fear, maybe trust. I chose to believe the second one.

I crouched just inside the doorway, bringing myself to eye level in case she chose to look up. I kept my distance, afraid pressing my luck might cause the girl to spring into the closet like a jackrabbit catching a glimpse of a coyote.

The second match wasn't ready to be put to pasture yet, but it was close, and the sudden return to darkness probably wouldn't bode well for the kid.

"Can you tell me your name?"

A shake of the head. Brisk and subtle, but definitely not a trick of the light.

"I told you from the hall, but I'm Rory. I used to live here. Matter of fact, this was my room. Now kid, we're gonna lose the light in a few seconds. Just givin' you the heads-up so it doesn't surprise you. When it shakes out, I'll light another one. That okay with you?"

A nod this time. Equally subtle, but we were communicating. That was good.

The light quivered, faded, and I worked quickly to deliver what I'd promised. When match number three chased the darkness away, she looked up at me. Her sunken eyes completed the picture of malnutrition, and I decided then and there I had to get this kid a meal. Come to think of it, I was about a day overdue for one myself.

"Sure you don't want to tell me your name so I don't have to keep calling you 'kid'?"

A rapid head shake disavowed me of that notion.

"Alright then kid, I'm goin' to head downstairs. Kinda hope you'll come with me, 'cause I'd feel guilty leaving you in the dark. There's nobody else downstairs; it's just the two of us in the house, so you ain't got to worry." I paused as something occurred to me. "Uh, there is a horse, but she won't bother you none."

The girl cocked her head and narrowed her eyes.

I almost added, "So, what do you say?" but the kid had made the answer to that question perfectly clear, so I gambled and stood tall, ready to walk out the door. Either the gunshot pops my knees gave off or the prospect of being resigned to the dark once more drew the girl to her feet lightning quick, blanket flying behind her like a cape. She followed the light like a damn moth, and we headed down to the first floor.

Pulling out a chair from the dining room table, I gestured for the kid to sit, which she did. I felt more than a little pride at the rapidly evolving trust between us.

"Alright, Pip, sit here a minute. I'm gonna try and relieve us of some of this darkness before these matches relieve my fingers of their skin. Then we'll find you some food."

Pip? Where the fuck did that come from?

I shrugged like I'd asked the question aloud, then set out to find something to pry the boards off the windows now that heat stroke, and its crippling headache, had passed by. The search didn't eat up much time. Whatever good Samaritan had done the bare minimum to safeguard my parents' house—saying it was mine still didn't feel right, though I suppose it was—had stacked the leftover materials in the parlor. Not altogether neatly, but in their defense, they probably figured it would be a while before anyone checked in on their work. Dust-covered boards, four-inch nails, a sturdy-looking hammer too nice to be forgotten, and a crowbar graced an empty corner of the room.

Making a mental inventory of the items in case they might be needed later, I wrapped my fingers around the crowbar and set to work. Nails squealed as I ripped them free against their will and each rusty scream brought a little bit of light into the world. I worked around the first floor, avoiding the dining room. If I could acclimate the kid to light a little bit at a time, maybe she wouldn't shrivel up and turn to dust when I got to the windows surrounding her.

I was in the process of liberating the kitchen when I felt eyes on me. A nervous chill at first—I'd been watched a little too often for my taste lately—but something about the feeling spoke of benevolence. For once, my company didn't mean me harm.

I turned with a smile, knowing I'd find the girl watching me. Hunger refused to let her wait any longer, or maybe she just wanted to see what I was up to. She squinted at the blinding sunrays but didn't slink away. The foyer still offered a little protection if she needed it. The smile I conjured for her faded quickly. She looked even more unhealthy in the light. I wondered, not for the first time, how the poor kid had ended up here. What circumstances could possibly lead to a child no more than eight being left to fend for themselves?

The irony wasn't lost on me.

"Come on," I said, an acknowledgement that the sun had enough points of entry for the time being. "I promised food."

The pantry wasn't empty. Far from it, in fact. I'd heard some foods taste better with age—wine and cheese, maybe—but if that was true for any consumables, it wasn't the ones William and Mae Daggett kept on hand.

"Uh, Pip. Looks like one or both of us needs to pick up some supplies. Seeing as you don't look so good, d'you wanna stay here? Hold down the fort?"

My dad used to say hold down the fort. That's the kind of thing only dads say.

She shook her head viciously, locks of dirty, stringy hair whipping from side to side to emphasize the point.

"Okay," I said, holding up my hand in concession. "You've spent enough time alone here. Don't want to spend any more.

I get that." I whispered the last bit. "But we're gonna have to make you presentable. Damn, kid, gonna have to make me presentable too."

We trooped out back and scouted out a few buckets. Most had succumbed to rust over the years, but a few evaded the elements. The spout filled them without complaint. Stationing ourselves on opposite sides of the yard, we washed up using some old hand towels from the kitchen. I swear I could feel my mom's eyes digging into the back of my shoulder blades every time I scrubbed. Backs turned to each other to preserve the little bit of modesty Pip's rags had left her, we toiled away to try and feel half human again.

I can't speak for the kid, but it worked wonders on me.

I wrapped my dripping body in a technically clean, but very musty, linen and offered one to Pip as well. To her credit, she didn't turn her nose up at it—nothing small considering she hadn't been born the last time it was washed.

Once inside, she showed a little hesitance to follow me back up the stairs, but I went up anyway, crowbar in hand to let my old bedroom breathe again. Cruel as it might sound, I knew she'd follow me if the alternative meant staying alone.

I wasn't wrong.

As we returned to the room I'd found her in, it struck me strange that she'd never entered the closet. If she had, more outfits than most kids owned in a lifetime would have waited to greet her. As she stood in the doorway, I made quick work of the temporary shutters so she could see the clothes she had to choose from.

"I'll leave you to get dressed. Pick anything you want and try it on. Might be a little loose on you, and, uh, they are boys' clothes, but they should fit more or less. You need anything, I'll be in the next room."

I left her staring at the closet, either in awe of the choices or held in place by the notion of moving forward. When my dad and I had lugged my stuff upstairs, I chose the biggest and best room, but I didn't need three, so one of them continued to serve as storage. The other I wasn't allowed in. Daddy always kept the door closed and on the rare occasion I snuck a peak, it appeared empty. There'd be clothes down in the master bedroom, but I wasn't quite ready to go there. Besides, William Daggett's pants fit a little more snugly when he died than mine did at twenty-three.

Stepping into the storage room, packed with clutter and a few chests, I eased through the labyrinth of history to get to the window. The boards squealed as I pried them loose from the window frames, and I made more racket than necessary, a way to remind the kid I was close. As the light poured in, exploring the long forgotten items, a certain chest caught my attention.

When I'd moved upstairs, the chest moved with me. Before then, it stood at the foot of my parents' bed. Ornately carved and decorated with some strange combination of floral patterns and runes, I used to spend hours running my fingers over the smooth wood, tracing the patterns etched into the surface. I opened it, relishing the familiar squeak of the hinges. Some things never changed and I guess that was alright.

Inside were my father's clothes, the ones that had grown a little too tight around the middle. I recall my mother insisting he get rid of them, but he swore up and down that they'd fit again someday. The extra weight around the middle was just a phase he was going through. Momma always joked most people called that phase denial, but the loving smile on her face said more than the words. So upstairs went the chest to be stored, until Daddy staved his paunch off or, well, until now.

Like old times, I walked my fingers over the fabric, letting them decide which I'd choose. Daddy had a knack for dressing sharp—or at least, Momma had that knack for him—so I couldn't go wrong. My searching hands found a pair of wool pants and a button-down shirt that would do the trick nicely. Like everything else in this house, they held onto a time-worn aroma, not unpleasant, but not something to strive for either. While that smell was the prevailing one, I couldn't miss a hint of the aftershave Daddy used to wear. Buried underneath the clothes, I found a holster, one I'd never seen him wear, since he didn't often carry a gun into town. If not for the initials WCD branded into the leather, I would've believed it belonged to someone else. I wrapped it around my middle and cinched it tight to complete the outfit, easing Henry Taff's blackened revolver into the holster. I don't know how long I stood in that room with a foolish grin on my face and a tear threatening to form at the corner of my eye, but it seemed like the sun moved, even if everything inside stayed still.

Eventually, I emerged from my reverie to go check on the kid. I half expected to find her still locked in a staredown with that closet, but she'd picked an outfit and looked a little less like grim death. The bath helped, her hair no longer a greasy mess, and the clothes hung off her as anticipated, but like me, she could pass for human in a social setting, and that was the goal.

McGregor's General still stood exactly the way I remembered it, positioned a little closer to the center of town to attract the right kind of clientele. The same could be said for Mr. McGregor, though the sides of his jet-black hair mingled with more gray than I recalled from previous visits.

"Help ya?" he barked without looking up from his work as Pip and I walked in the front. A few other shoppers went about their business, no doubt used to the shopkeeper's brusque manner.

"Uh, yeah, maybe." My face felt hot. I'd gotten us ready and all the way here before realizing I didn't have any money. "I don't suppose my family's line of credit is any good still?"

His pencil strokes filled the space his voice didn't want to touch. I never thought of Herschel McGregor as kind nor cruel when I was younger, just there. I don't believe he let the question linger out of any kind of malice, though the lack of an answer felt decidedly like a no. The pencil made its final mark and he laid it to rest, letting out a sigh.

"And what family name would that be, sir?"

"Daggett." I said it with a little more timidity than I meant to. Like dropping it into conversation was something I was out of practice with.

McGregor's head raised so slowly, a looming creak wouldn't have sounded out of place. "Daggett?" he asked like he'd misheard. "Rory. Oh my Lord, I haven't seen you since the . . ." He cleared his throat. When he resumed, his words came with hesitance. "Well, in a long time. How are you? What brings you in?"

While delivering his rambling horde of questions, he studied every inch of me visible over the countertop, searching for evidence to the contrary of who I said I was. The surprise was genuine, though, and it was nice to speak with someone who both talked back and didn't work for Holcomb. God, I hoped he didn't work for Holcomb.

"Well, Mr. McGregor, I've been better, but I've been worse too. I'm, uh, in the process of movin' back home. Fixin' up the house. Thing is we've got nothin' to eat and until I scrounge around deep enough, I've got nothin' to pay for it with."

I fought my cheeks turning red again and thought of Henry Taff. If the man had taught me nothing else—and he'd taught me a lot—he'd instilled that it was okay not to be well-off and there was no shame in a man asking for help when he truly needed it.

McGregor didn't make me wait as long for an answer this time, though he nodded while he sought out the proper words. When he found them, they spilled out with a tone something like embarrassment. Men who owned shops in this part of town generally didn't align with Taff's credo. "Sure, Rory, take what you need. We'll settle up later. I know you're good for it." An awkward pause followed, like something else occupied his mind. "That your daughter?"

Goddamn, I'd almost forgotten about the kid, following me around quiet as a mouse fart. I turned to check on her and sure enough, Pip waited dutifully behind me, making sensual eye contact with every edible item in sight.

"No, Pip is . . ."

Pip is what? I couldn't very well tell him I'd found a homeless kid and was now in the act of dragging her around the more scenic areas of Buzzard's Edge. It didn't ring as illegal, but it surely was odd.

McGregor furrowed his brow, acknowledging the suspicious amount of time I'd taken to locate the end of the sentence.

". . . a cousin," I finished, in a tone that didn't usually accompany the truth.

"Pip, huh? Alright," said McGregor. His voice said he didn't believe me, but he didn't particularly care.

I changed the subject before McGregor could change his mind about his offered generosity. "Really appreciate you helping us out, Herschel."

He winced at my use of his first name. "Think nothing of it. Your parents always treated me well." He paused again, though the look on his face said he wasn't searching for words. He knew exactly what he wanted to say, just had to weigh the delicacy first. "I miss them, Rory."

"Yeah," I said, feeling my throat constrict. "Yeah, me too."

He nodded, our conversation approaching its natural end. "When you get what you need, just bring it up here so I can note it down."

"Sure thing, Mr. McGregor."

The shop owner hadn't balked at extending me a line of credit based solely on my last name. It carried meaning with the town's people and I determined to grab just enough stores to get Pip and me through a few days. We'd come back for more when we could pay off that debt. Or maybe we'd move on by then. I truly did not know what tomorrow held.

We filled our arms with canned preserves, vegetables, beans, some fresh baked bread, and a small side of beef from the butcher's section, enough for a single meal. I didn't recall whether the house had an icebox and didn't want to deprive the other patrons of meat only to let it go to waste. I bore the brunt of the load, not trusting Pip's skinny arms to carry more than one or two items. As we placed them on the counter in as orderly a fashion as possible, McGregor retrieved his pencil from behind his ear and set to writing out a receipt.

I'd only had eyes for food while traveling around the store, but with that need on its way to being satiated, I took in the people in the sparsely populated general store. A pair of mothers, gathering items with one hand and wrangling children far more unruly than Pip with the other, garnered most of the attention. An older gentleman scanned the shelves without a care in the world. Nowhere to be for days, most likely, and he'd find what he needed or he wouldn't. No skin off his back.

Another customer surveyed the fruit, the non-canned stuff. Time stopped as I took in the long black dress. At least black was the first color that sprang to mind, but really it was the lack of color, absorbing the essence of anything with the temerity to come in contact with it. The curls in her hair looked familiar. I hadn't dwelled on them last time because her twisting fingers stole my attention, contorting into evil signs and laying waste to my agency, but it was the same woman. He'd sent Merella to spy on me, finish the job she'd started at the ranch, which meant Dorrance hid in wait somewhere. Maybe inside the store, maybe right outside, prepared to kick my ass once more. They'd already murdered Willie. This time they'd take the kid. Sweat poured from my brow and my heart sped up as I searched the store for any hiding spot large enough to conceal Dorrance, while also keeping watch on Merella, lest she drift away into nothingness. The crone made to move from the produce, spin around and place a curse on me, so I drew my gun as quick as I had on Edwards. Quicker, even, and pointed it directly into the face of a harmless old woman.

My breathing sped up and I began to panic as she dropped an armload of apples to the ground. The spilled fruit resulted in a series of knocks that drew the eyes of everyone in the store. They screamed when they saw my gun drawn. The little old woman burst into tears. She wore a deep purple dress, not black, and her dark silver hair hung with nary a curl in sight. Her wide, glistening eyes saw me as some rogue outlaw who abandoned his usual round of bank robberies and high noon duels to rob the grocery allowance from a poor old widow.

I tried to apologize, but it stuck in my throat. The best I could do was jam the gun back in its holster and shake my head, hoping she might understand this was all a mistake. She was never in any danger.

Except she was.

I grabbed Pip by the hand and pulled her to the counter, gathering up our items. McGregor's jaw hung open so wide it was a wonder he kept his tongue contained. The shock present and unhidden on the lower half of his face didn't extend to his eyes. A mix of anger and disappointment lived in those eyes as they watched me approach the counter. He didn't have to tell me I didn't live up to the Daggett name.

I had no way of knowing whether he'd finished totaling our groceries. Scooping them up, I half-shouted an assemblage of syllables I hoped resembled 'thank you' and shuffled out the door.

The house we'd come from didn't feel like home yet, but it felt a damn sight more hospitable than the choking and judgmental atmosphere we were fleeing from. Pip and I ran from the storefront, dropping more than one or two items on the way, and drawing a multitude of strange looks.

Turning back to check for any kind of pursuit, I caught the eye of the old widow. She stood in front of McGregor's General, Herschel McGregor by her side, scowling and with hands on his hips. Her dress remained purple and her hair stayed straight and silver, but her tears had dried up.

She was smiling. By her side, her pale fingers wriggled like worms.

CHAPTER 9

DRAWING LINES IN THE DUST

The house, or manor, as the rest of Buzzard's Edge referred to it, drew our eyes from some distance away. Prominent as it was, it stood out like a beacon. I still felt dizzy from the events at the general store, any logical thought eroded away, but deep down, reason still told me the house wasn't atop a hill, looming over the townspeople in a condescending way. That's just the way it seemed; a presence lording over the town, dormant for years, but now very much awake again. And I'd done that.

Entering the foyer, the natural light stopped me in my tracks. The house felt somehow warmer. Dust motes floated lazily among the sun's rays, like carrion birds trying to spot prey. Would they zip down if they saw something appetizing? Aside from the dust, it looked like home again. Pip studied me, unsure why I'd frozen a few steps inside the door. She didn't ask and that was alright, because I didn't have an answer that would make sense.

My legs unlocked and we trooped into the dining room, our temporary base of operations. Our haul took up a lot less space on the table than its heft suggested, but it would do in the short term. Scratching at my chin, I studied the loot, trying to figure out what to make. Easy choice. Beans on a tortilla. Something that would fill us up and not be too tough on the taste buds either. I'd get some vegetables into the kid later.

The kitchen never felt like part of the home, if I'm honest, which I attributed to not being allowed in there. It made sense, as much as being barred from any area of your own house does. The dining room existed for dining, the only thing that people tend to do with food when they have as much money in the bank as William and Mae Daggett did. The kitchen is for preparing food, something the citizens in the center of Buzzard's Edge hadn't done themselves for a long time, if ever. At least I could say I was proud William Daggett worked for his stock, as opposed to the others born with a silver spoon hanging out the corner of their toothless, spittle-covered maws. A stove sat in the corner, but I didn't know what to make of it. The Taffs, who taught me self sufficiency, cooked over the hearth. I'd use what I knew and leave the exploration for another day when I wasn't starving half to death. As I set the wood—still just fine after all this time, maybe even more dried out and suited to the job—a twinge of guilt struck over my own hunger. The kid stood closer to starvation than I ever had. Her arms and legs resembled kindling, her skin functioning as a simple adornment for the jutting bones underneath. We'd cook the beans straight in the can, no scraping out ancient cookware for us. I set the can above the glowing hearth and set down to watch it heat up.

Letting out a deep sigh, I tried the kid again. "Why won't you talk to me?"

Her eyes, previously fixed on the impending meal, dropped to the dust-laden ground and she shook her head.

A notion struck, almost like a candle illuminating a portion of my mind I hadn't visited before, buried in shadows as it was. "Pip, can you talk?"

She shook her head again and the previous hours of the day roared into focus. I couldn't see where the path ahead went, but at least one existed and it wasn't completely overgrown.

"Okay then, progress. So we keep it to yes or no questions. Let's see. Well, I'm gonna assume your name isn't really Pip, though it does fit. Right?"

The girl shook her head and held up a bony index finger. On the dusty floorboard in front of her, she drew, moving the dust around to reveal clean wood underneath. One painstaking character at a time, her true name revealed itself.

A-L-I-C-E.

"Alice," I said. "Well, it's real nice to formally meet you. Would you hate me terribly if I slipped and called you Pip every so often?"

A smile graced her face, the first I'd seen, and my heart about lit up at the sight of it. I'd heard the adage that making children smile was God's gift to the world, but until I discovered the ability to carve a chunk of happiness on that granite block of a face, those were just words. "So Pi— Alice. You know your letters, but you can't speak. A conundrum, as a great man I once knew used to say." That was Henry. In addition to not displaying any shame when he needed a helping hand financially, the man had no problem admitting when he couldn't answer a question; an admirable trait.

"Has it always been like this for you?"

Another nod. I had so many questions that wouldn't fit neatly into a yes or no box. The writing opened things up a little, but the floor only contained so much dust.

"What happened to the people who took care of you? Your parents?" I knew it couldn't be answered simply, but the question slipped out anyway. Alice must have come to the same realization because she didn't shake, nod, or extend an index finger. Just looked up and met my gaze, like I could find the answers in her eyes if I only knew how to look. Her eyes were the same shade of blue as the clearest lake you ever saw. I took up the challenge and studied them, but that particular mystery didn't see fit to reveal itself. Not that day, anyway. After a few false starts to the next question, I arrived at what I wanted to say, but the fifth draft didn't sound any less crazy than the first.

"You see anything funny when we were at the store? Before I nearly shot an old woman, that is. Anything strike you as odd?"

Alice cocked her head thoughtfully, no doubt replaying the events that led to our emergency egress. A moment passed before she nodded. Her nods had every bit as much character as most kids put into their words. I'd seen the fast, fervent ones that betrayed excitement about something, and those were easiest to read. This one moved slow, not like she was unsure—more like she didn't know if she should answer. When her head returned to its initial position, she lifted one hand, shook her fingers as if warming them in front of the hearth and then drew a series of complex geometric shapes in the air. At first I thought letters, but not any letters I knew.

Regardless of the shapes, my gut chilled, sharing a sneaking suspicion of what—or who—the writhing fingers represented. I pondered a follow-up question, but the heavenly smell of cooked beans derailed my train of thought, so I made a note to circle back around later.

With the food served up, we dug in with a feverish intensity. No one else was present, and we'd become accustomed to each other's company enough to eat like animals. Ghost knickered softly from the other room. We'd need to go back to the ranch at some point today, get her something to eat, and take care of the other animals as well.

Somewhere between burritos three and four, a knock on the door interrupted our meal. Alice's eyes went wide and her lunch hit the floor with a soft plop. It would have struck me funny if she didn't look so terrified. Clearly, the kid had a lot more to tell me. I wasn't immune to her panic, but it didn't hit me as hard, mostly because I had an inkling who was on the other side of that knock. I just didn't care to talk about the reason that brought them here.

"Need to go upstairs and hide, Pip," I whispered. "Quiet as you can pull off."

She chewed frantically and swallowed with an audible gulp, arguing with those icy blue eyes all the while.

"Easier this way, kid. I swear up and down by the man Jesus himself, I won't leave you, but shit's a whole lot less . . . complicated if you're out of sight for a few."

She disagreed—made that clear when she narrowed her eyes with a pouty kind of anger—but picked up the burrito, dusted it off, and started toward the stairs. A second set of knocks, these ones carrying a bit more urgency, almost made her drop it again.

"Yep, I'm on my way," I called, never dropping my eyes from hers. Not until she disappeared to the second floor. I gave Pip—no, Alice— a minute to settle before I got up to answer the door, checking for the gun still tucked in my father's holster. Just in case I was mistaken about who'd come looking for me.

With my hand resting on the butt, I opened the door, nearly blinded by the gleam coming off the shiny sheriff's badge. Squinting, my eyes climbed to his unsmiling face. I read the room and dispensed with the bullshit, peering over his shoulder dramatically to set the scene for my story.

"Well, I guess you better come in, John."

"Sorry to interrupt your lunch," said John Harden, heading toward the kitchen. His tone didn't sound overly sorry.

"No spectacular feast, this. You hungry?"

"I'll pass, thank you." He avoided looking at me, passing his gaze around the room as though he might discover something to keep him from having to say his piece. I allotted him all the time in the world, determined not to speak first. "Those your daddy's clothes?"

Taken aback, I couldn't manage anything past a nod.

"Look good on you. I'm, uh, more'n a little surprised to see you back here. Not displeased, don't get me wrong. Just unexpected is all." He sighed. "I s'pose you know why I'm here."

"I can think of a couple potentials. Why don't you help me narrow it down."

"Fair enough. I been looking for you most of the morning. Half-thought you might've succumbed to the flames. Ain't nothin' left of the ranch 'cept some freestanding stables and a few unruly animals. Tom Corley agreed to look after 'em 'til further notice. Employed Timmy to help him out."

"Good kid."

"Yeah," he said absently, looking around again. "What we did not find was any evidence of you or Willie. Sent me into a bit of a panic, if I'm to stay honest." He cocked an eyebrow and waited.

"Wasn't much left of Willie to bury. I guess you wouldn't have found her unless you knew where to look." After I said it, I realized how suspicious it sounded. If Harden heard some cause in there, he didn't let on.

"Left me scratchin' my head, too. Until Mr. McGregor asked for my ear." He raised his eyebrow once more. "Know what he said?"

Safer not to answer this one, so I shook my head.

"Well, he said a man claiming to be Rory Daggett held one of his customers at gunpoint and then robbed him of a hefty supply of groceries. Some beans included," he added, inclining his head toward the empty can on the floor.

"Doesn't that fuckin' beat all," I said, more to myself. "Guess he forgot the part where he agreed to let me have that food on credit."

"Jesus, Rory, it's true?" He reached up to remove his hat, give his head a little air to cool off. "Maybe it slipped his mind when you threatened to blow an old woman's head off."

"Did he tell you the old woman's name?"

"What the Christ does that have to do with anything?"

"Bet he didn't know it," I said. He didn't need to answer. I saw it on his face.

I studied Harden, the closest thing I had to a friend since the day Noose executed my parents, the only person on that train platform who saw me as anything more than a bloody reminder of the town's greed coming back to haunt it. I sighed as I made up my mind to confide in him. If I couldn't trust John Harden, I was lost anyway.

"You want to hear my side, or you just goin' to invoke the Lord until he rides down on a white horse?"

His cheeks reddened, either from anger or embarrassment, and he gestured for me to talk so his voice wouldn't reveal which one. We sat for damn near an hour while I filled the sheriff in on just about every second between our post-Crane conversation at Lynch's and the current moment, only leaving Alice out of the conversation. Seemed like the type of thing a law man would need to take action on, and I didn't care to put him in that unenviable position. Besides, she didn't change the story's trajectory all that much.

Harden reacted as any engaged audience might, and at all the appropriate parts. He looked properly horrified when the story got to Dorrance's appearance, displayed a mix of dubious disbelief and surprise at Merella's magic—I'd suspected he hadn't believed me when I'd told him before; his raised eyebrows only confirmed that notion—and all but plugged his ears when I got to the part about a knife-wielding felon buried in the back garden. That part was key, though. I couldn't convince him I'd encountered the witch picking up groceries without those cursory details that tied it all together. He didn't blink at what I'd encountered at McGregor's.

Finished, I let him soak in the dregs of the tale. He appeared out of his depth, unsure how the fuck a sane man, never mind a man of law and order, should react. He'd watched my face, but dropped his gaze when the last words met his ears, avoiding stimuli while digesting the truth.

Following a lengthy silence, he spoke. "Who's Alice?"

Harden's eyes led mine to the floorboard still displaying the kid's name. I thought about lying, and I'm pretty sure he saw that. "Come on, Rory. You think anyone's going to leave out the detail about a kid being an accomplice to an armed robbery?"

"That's not—"

"Fine, she tricked you. The witch. Tell me about the kid."

"Not much to tell." I kept my eyes on the well-formed letters, drawn by pencil-thin fingers. The lack of eye contact was the telltale sign of a liar, but I expected I had him wrapped up by now. "Found her upstairs when I arrived, abandoned and malnourished. No idea how long she lived here, but she was pale as the day is long, skinny as a fuckin' stick, and grimy. I cleaned her up and dressed her. She seemed too scared to stay alone, so I brought her to McGregor's to get something to feed her. Had I known they'd come after me again—and I should've known that, John—I would've insisted she stay behind."

"You ask her who left her here and when?"

Information I'd worked hard for, now about to be shared so freely, brought a smirk to my face. "She can't talk."

"Can't or won't?"

"Won't because she can't." I shrugged.

Harden breathed out in a huff, sat staring at me like time had stilled. I met his eyes, waiting for him to speak first. I'd exhausted my stock of words.

After a moment of sitting so still I hadn't even registered a blink, Harden spoke up, causing me to jump. "Here's what we're gonna do, hoss. I'm gonna tell McGregor about the fire at the ranch." He held up a hand, stopping my objection in its tracks. "He don't need to know how the fire started or any other gritty details. Just that you was under considerable stress today and you had a, whatchamacallit . . . an event, we'll say. He won't be satisfied, and you should probably stay the fuck away from that store, but that's what happened." He pressed his lips together, a firm stance as if I were McGregor prepared to argue the point.

"And the kid?"

"I didn't see no kid here." He sighed as he got to his feet, replacing his hat on his balding dome. "Searched the whole house and everything. McGregor must have seen someone else's kid and thought they was with you."

I grinned, couldn't help it. "I told him it was my cousin."

A big inhale. "Well, fuck him anyway, I guess. Always did have a stick five feet up his ass."

He made for the door and I got up to follow him. "John, I appreciate your confidence more than I can say. I really do."

"Those are the words of a man who's about to ask for another favor, Rory."

"I'm close. I got two of Holcomb's guys, and I can feel him sniffing around the corner. Toying with me, yeah, but he's close. Think how much it would mean to the people of Buzzard's Edge to get them free from the grip of this boogeyman."

"He ain't been seen for fifteen years, kid. You know that better'n anybody."

"And people forgot about him? You go back to the general store and mention his name, the folk down there are just gonna brush it off? You don't believe that."

"No, I guess I don't." Concern filled his eyes. I'd asked too much of him already that day, and still knew he'd say yes to any request. When Harden pulled me off the train way back when, he saved my life, in a manner of speaking. When someone saves your life, they feel responsible for you. They'll bend over backwards and break any rules they can get away with to see that things turn out alright. I almost wish I didn't know that.

"Be there when I call for you," I said. "That's it. I'll find these fuckers and when I do, I'm gonna need backup."

"Shit Rory, that sounds like the job of the sheriff anyway."

"We ain't bringing them in alive."

He stared for another moment, no disagreement in his eyes. It was more like he needed to study me to see if I had the mettle. I sure as hell hoped I did.

"I might know a guy who could help." John offered a slight nod, then walked out the door, shutting it behind him.

I hadn't even started toward the stairs when a familiar voice broke the peace.

"Daggett!" it roared like rolling thunder, creeping through the floorboards and shooting up through my body to make my arm hair stand on end. I knew that voice. Heard it the day before, in fact. I threw open the door before I could consider how much smarter barricading it might be, and found Dorrance down by the hitching post, holding Harden by the back of the neck like an ill-behaved tomcat. Harden's legs kicked the air inches above the ground, trying to find purchase.

"He comes when he's called. What a good boy. Maybe try not to piss yourself this time." Well-rested and not choking on smoke, I heard his voice clearly; Two boulders, so massive only a god could budge them, scraped together. Something that usually happened at a glacial pace sped up until it formed words, or something like them.

Harden's voice demanded my attention, sounding considerably more human. "Get back inside!" was all he could muster before Dorrance gave him a shake, flinging the sheriff's body forward as though he intended to throw him, then snapping him back at the last moment. Harden's head and limbs jolted with such force, I'm not sure how his neck didn't break.

I should have heeded his words, but remained frozen in the doorway. Mostly frozen, anyway. My right hand inched toward the holster to retrieve the gun. I could still feel the weight tugging at my hip. Dorrance returned Harden to the scruffed cat position. The sheriff's arms and legs hung listlessly as a hanged man, a sight Harden knew well. With his prey no longer trying to escape, Dorrance struck up a big grin, splitting his butt-ugly mug from ear to ear. It didn't appear happy, amused, or even cruel. Just horrible.

I drew the revolver and lined up a shot to put out one of his beady little eyes. As quickly as I went, he lifted Harden like a shield before I could pull the trigger, swinging the man around like he weighed no more than the gun drawing down on him.

"Put it down, Daggett. Else you ain't gon' like what happens to your friend here."

Harden was probably dead the moment he walked out the door. I despised myself for thinking in terms like that, but that's how it was. Only way I wouldn't join him was if I properly employed the element of surprise.

So I shot Dorrance in the foot.

As soon the revolver kicked I burst forward, hoping to take advantage and get the big man off his balance. I caught myself partway down the path and skidded to a stop. He hadn't budged. I cursed my aim, then realized the newfound hole in his boot was spurting blood. Worst of all, he laughed about it, a deep hellish sound that wouldn't bring a smile to passersby like good laughter should. Rather, the kind that haunts your dreams.

"Try again," he bellowed. "Put the gun down and kick it over here."

I didn't much care for the idea, but I'd put a bullet in him and he'd still spared my friend. Maybe there was a happy ending possible after all. I dropped the revolver and kicked it with the side of my boot, about halfway between us but a little closer to him.

"And put them hands up."

I complied, still ready to spring at a second's notice.

Another bout of laughter. "Good."

He dropped Harden, and I sighed with relief. It was short-lived. What I'd mistaken for the release of a hostage was something far worse. Harden's exhausted body fell next to the hitching post, his head leaned against it at the perfect angle for what this gigantic asshole had planned. Dorrance lifted his boot and brought it down with the force of a hundred horses, trapping Harden's skull between boot and wood. The boot pressed forward. The skull and the wood both gave way, the sickening crunch of each indistinguishable from the other.

It happened so fast, I couldn't muster a reaction until shards of bone and splinters of wood, clumped together with blood and brain, decorated my clothes from head to toe.

Dorrance inspected his work and when he saw no second shot was necessary, he shook the detritus from his foot.

Fury took over at the expense of good sense and I charged the giant, running right past the revolver on the ground. I threw left hooks and right crosses. I emptied my arsenal, every move that William Daggett and Henry Taff ever taught me, and a few I'd learned on my own. Each one met a firm wall. I'd hit men before and even the biggest and toughest had a give to them. This was no man, but a force of nature. He took every blow I dealt, displaying no more reaction than when I'd shot him in the foot. When my logical brain tried to take the controls back from my animal brain, a single word shone through the murk.

Balls.

I ceased my assault and smiled up at him. His laughter, a low rumble of background noise, had been a constant, but when Dorrance caught my grin, his own dropped. I swung my right leg forward with everything I had, planting the kick firmly between his legs. Even the toughest men in the world couldn't push on with a pair of mashed testicles.

The opening I sought finally materialized as the massive tree of a man crashed to the packed dirt road with a concussive bang that shook the strangely deserted neighborhood. I pounced on Dorrance, delivering blows to the parts that tended to end fights the quickest: the bridge of the nose, his eyes, and throat. Finding himself the prey—and I imagine he wasn't used to that situation—Dorrance put his testicular torture to the back of his mind and focused on getting me off his head. He spun on the ground like an unbroke stallion, writhing and trying to crush my ass. Every time I narrowly avoided finding myself under his body weight, I considered how it exceeded mine by at least double. Come to think of it, the same thrashing that almost squashed me like a flapjack caused him to lose that eye.

I scratched at his face, banishing all notions of a fair fight from my vocabulary. As my pointer finger raked his eye, he spun away, causing my finger to hook the socket like a fish biting down on a baited line.

The eyeball came free with a wet popping sound that stirred up the beans in my stomach. I quickly forgot that feeling when Dorrance unleashed a piercing scream and increased his floundering. The man had made my acquaintance twice, and though he didn't strike me as a big talker, his voice and laughter played in the range of the bassoon from that unfinished symphony Edwards harped on about. This scream, shredding the man's vocal cords before arriving at my ear, more closely resembled a pocket cornet in volume, pitch, and overall shrillness—a truly unpleasant instrument.

As he continued to flail about, the thought of the loose revolver returned to mind. I sprinted for it. Almost had it before my legs went out from under me. The ground rose up and slammed into my face. I assumed I'd tripped until a pressure around my ankle dragged me away from the revolver as it lay just an arms' length away. I watched it recede into the distance, wishing I'd run with a little more purpose as Dorrance grabbed the back of my neck. Scruffing grown men like stray cats was evidently the big fucker's signature move.

My gorge rose again when he lifted me to meet him eye-to-eye, or what now passed for that. His hateful right eye remained in place, a mean streak too big to be contained within a smaller man on full display. The left eye was the problem.

Technically it was intact, but it hung a couple inches lower than usual, resting upon his scruffy cheek and staring distantly through me. The eyeball held on by a single thread of . . . whatever the fuck keeps eyeballs from falling out of a person's head on a good day. I can't imagine a circumstance that would have made the sight comical, but the grimace etched on his face left no doubt about his anger.

My eyes darted to Harden's corpse, still resting against the fence, and I suspected I'd be joining him shortly. He didn't appear to have suffered, but I'd only traveled two-fifths of the way down the vengeance trail. Not that I was some fierce warrior, but I'd expected to get more than halfway.

When Dorrance gave my suspended body a harsh shake, I must have gotten a distant look in my eye, pondering my end. I returned my attention to his disfigured mug, trying not to focus on the eyeball pendulum.

"Had orders to bring you in roughed up but alive, Daggett. He didn't say what roughed up meant exactly, but he sent me, didn't he? Probably figured I'd drag your ass in bleeding from every orifice. Maybe minus an arm or somethin'."

Dorrance didn't specify who he was, but he didn't have to. I knew, and he knew I knew.

"But this," he continued, gesturing to his eye. "This, I can't abide. It's a shame things got out of hand." He pulled me closer, his breath a mix of rot and blood, and forced me to admire my own handiwork. My hands hung limp by my side. I might get one chance to take a shot and I wanted it to count. Maybe take that other eye, wipe the nasty bugger right off his face. Something brushed my right hand as I waited for the opportunity to present itself.

"Way I see it, Daggett, I tried like hell to knock you senseless, but you're a wily one. Took out Edwards with barely a scratch. I can see we underestimated you."

There it was again. A light tug at my right hand, then gone. I didn't dare look away from Dorrance. He might decide he'd talked enough and snap my neck then and there.

" 'Oh Noose, I didn't mean to,' " he said, affecting an airy voice at odds with his normal timbre. " 'Truly I didn't, but the little fucker tripped and fell running away. Landed on his neck just so. And crack.' "

He squeezed my neck as he said it, emphasizing the threat. I waited for another touch, but when it came, it was different. Something pressed into my palm. I squeezed it and felt my anonymous benefactor hand the weight over to me. I couldn't be sure of the item without a peek, but I had a pretty good idea of what I now held, and who had slipped it to me.

Quiet as a mouse fart.

"Course he might not believe me, but—" Dorrance stopped mid-thought and scrunched up his face, which only emphasized the empty eye socket, now oozing a bloody foam. "What in the everlovin' fuck are you smiling about?" Holding his arm out straight, he dangled me at length, as though the smile I'd let slip might be contagious as cholera. Dorrance caught sight of my gift a split second too late. By then, I'd already let it swing and watched with a nasty sort of glee as the hammer's claw tore into the side of his head.

Never one to take unnecessary chances, I yanked it free, pulling a sizable chunk of skull out with it, and buried it into the crown of his head. I'd shoveled a lot of horse shit in my time, and the most bothersome part of this attack wasn't the sight of the skull caving in. It was the way the hammer meeting head sounded like a shovel digging into manure. His sausage-like fingers dug into the back of my neck, but I was three hits deep by then and attributed the action to a sort of death throe more than him fighting back. Those days were over for Dorrance.

His grip still held me inches off the ground as I laid waste to his skull, a sculptor molding clay into some unrecognizable abomination. His brain died long before his legs got the message, but when they did, we collapsed in a bloody heap.

The street begged for a healthy dose of rain to wash away the blood, bone, brains, and hate spilled that day, but this was Buzzard's Edge. Even in the best part of town, the sand would drink the blood and unloved creatures would dispose of the rest when darkness fell. Except for the hate. That would stay indefinitely.

I rolled out from underneath Dorrance's behemoth corpse and tossed the hammer to the center of the street, not wanting anything more to do with it. I'd buy a new one if it came down to it. When I didn't see Alice immediately, I feared the giant might have fallen on her, but she appeared from behind me before that terror could sink its teeth in.

"You saved my ass, Pip."

She smiled, then looked down at her feet. Almost like the scene was too grim to bring any joy. I hated watching life steal that away from her.

I hoisted myself up, not feeling nearly as broken as I should have for battling Goliath without a slingshot. "Let's go inside."

I picked up the revolver off the ground, then Alice caught my eye. She looked from me to the mess in the street. Her meaning was clear.

Ain't you gonna clean up after yourself?

"Fuck," I mumbled.

Two more for the backyard.

CHAPTER 10

FIREPOWER AND CLARITY

Carrying John Harden's body to the backyard of Daggett Manor felt wrong in every conceivable way. I couldn't leave him out front to rot under the sun; couldn't bring him inside, either. I took a little solace in burying him away from where I'd put Edwards, where I would put Dorrance. A velvet mesquite provided a reasonable facsimile of shade in one corner of the yard. I buried him there, deep enough that a determined critter couldn't get to him without a fight. They'd be forced to settle for the spoiled meat closer to the surface.

With the work finished, I said a short goodbye to my friend while Alice watched from the shade.

Dorrance caused my body more strain in death than he had in life. Alice, somewhere south of ten years old and so skinny her bones just about clanked when she walked, didn't add much to the effort. She tried to help haul Dorrance's body, but in the end, I recruited Ghost and let her drag his heavy ass. Even then, the going was slow and the reluctant mare huffed in an exasperated manner as she pulled. On a positive note, she seemed happy to be outside again.

The gritty soil covering Edwards's remains hadn't settled yet, making it easy to find a place to put Noose's plus-sized henchman. It was less work to identify the spot than to dig the hole, but we managed.

By the time the sheriff and the giant were in the ground, the setting sun bled a mixture of pink and purple so vivid, it looked more like a painter's palette than the hellish sky that had overseen this day. With the sunset came the cool, and as nice as the chill felt at first, we quickly retreated inside.

"Got us a problem, Pip. Maybe a whole host of 'em."
She held up a finger, drawing the letter A in the air.
"Alice, right. Sorry, kid. That's gonna take some getting used to."
She nodded her head, likely more out of sympathy than an understanding of our current state—my current state anyway—but I appreciated the ear.
Ticking off a single finger, I started listing the problems. If I said them out loud, they'd manifest in reality, and hopefully some far-fetched solution would occur to me.
"The sheriff of Buzzard's Edge is buried in the backyard. Mr. Harden back there was the closest thing I had to a friend—that honor falls to you now," I added, shooting Alice a grin. "There's folks that know we were close, but then he came here to talk to a man acting erratically in public. I didn't know any better, I might think Noose set the thing up on purpose. Shit, kid. I guess I don't know better."
Alice held up two fingers, prompting me to continue.
"Okay, okay. Problem number two. Because of problem number one, we need to act sooner than later. Like before the town even knows Harden is missing." I held up a third finger.
"Tied on like a fuckin' bow to problem number two is that we don't know what to do, where to go next. So far, this merry gang of assholes has tracked me down, and they all keep dying before I can ask 'em anything."

I flashed a glance at Alice, but her expression betrayed nothing. I'd talked myself in a circle and had nothing to show for it. "Only one that shared anything was that fool Crane, but he had such a taste of his own medicine by then, I don't see that we can put much stock in it. Cavern." I tasted the word, bland and unhelpful as it rolled around on my tongue. "Cavern."

I let it linger a moment, hoping it would ignite something it hadn't before. "Ah fuck, know what, Alice? That man of science was so fucked up by the end, I could barely understand a word. Might've been something else. Going on about badgers or something. Maybe he was asking for a ladder. Or . . ."

Alice cocked her head. She'd seen the answer flash in my eyes. Hell, I felt it, like fire racing through my brain. Not badgers or ladders or even adders. Tavern. All the places to hide in the desert, I heard what I wanted to hear. Noose and the witch. They were hiding right here in town.

"The tavern, kid. Saint's a-fuckin'-live. Lynch's Tavern." Thoughts filled my head like stars dotting the night. There were too many to count and they all tried to shine at once. Alice's face embodied patience. Sucking in a deep breath, I tried to sort the funnel of ideas into a single-file line, but rage boiled just under the surface. I hated myself for not figuring it out sooner. Harden could've lived. Willie would still be at the ranch. Hell, I would be too.

"The sheriff and I celebrated with a drink at that very tavern, same day we took down the first member of their crew. The rest of them were probably hidin' in some back room. Shit, maybe even watching us." My skin crawled at that notion, and I let a tick go by, hoping time might alleviate the feeling.

"We gotta move, Alice." I met her eyes and she nodded. "It's a massive ask, my friend, but will you come with me?"

A second nod.

"They'll probably know I'm coming. Might even know I got a kid with me. This town always did do its share of talking." I stared at the revolver, deeming it cruelly insufficient, but it was all I had. I'd buried Harden with his own iron, and I wasn't about to go ask for it back. Alice studied the charred pistol, then popped to her feet, flying halfway up the stairs before I could even furrow my brow at the curious action. I leapt up and followed, chasing her past my old room, turning away from the storage room and coming to a rest before the third doorway. Closed, like always. Off limits.

"What—" I started to ask, but Alice barged in and crossed the room, making straight for the closet. She threw the door open to reveal nothing more than dust, cobwebs, and a few pissed off spiders—items the house held in spades. Her face impassive, she entered and began rustling around inside, rattling around and sounding like a muffled stampede on a hardwood floor. The banging stopped following a sustained groaning creak. Alice emerged carrying a large board, one that eclipsed her entire upper half, with her fingers stuck in knot holes. She jerked her head, encouraging me to look inside. Before I could understand exactly what I was looking at, light spilled in the window and reflected off an item in the closet's depths.

"Motherfucker." The word rolled past my slack jaw. I figured my dad must have had an armory somewhere in the house, but the stores in here rivaled what Harden kept at the sheriff's office. Might have even outshined it. Hard to believe I'd slept right down the hall from all this firepower most of my life.

I turned to Alice and she flashed a grin, one that transformed the quiet mouse I'd come to know over the last twenty-four hours. Mischief lived in this one, alright, and that streak might come in handy.

"Been a long fuckin' day, Alice. A long fuckin' day. Be suicide to try and find them tonight. Probably not a great idea to stay here, but we're gonna load up, eat up, get a little shut-eye, and one way or another, put this thing behind us tomorrow. That sound like a plan to you?"

She nodded. No hesitation, nerves or otherwise. I suspect trust or loyalty was a foreign concept to the girl, but she felt it toward me, and I toward her. We'd take care of each other, and after tomorrow, Noose would never fuck with us again.

Chapter 11

The Last Train to Buzzard's Edge

The kid slept well, and I must have nodded off once or twice, but I remember the bulk of the night crawling by. We'd raided the armory, taken just enough for me to carry without getting weighed down. I grabbed the bullet I'd saved from the train and again from the burning farmhouse, and loaded it into Henry's revolver—my revolver—by its lonesome. I might not know what the bullet's purpose was yet, but I meant to have it on me when I found out.

Alice looked strangely at home handling weapons, leaving me to guess whether she had experience in her former life or used that closet as a playroom in her time here. The situation was fraught enough—three corpses in the yard and a storekeeper who half wanted me strung up—so we opted to forego target practice out back.

We kept breakfast light, not wanting to puke from the nerves that came with strolling to your own death. When neither of us could find anything else that needed to be done, we walked Ghost out the front door to meet the empty morning street. Four, five times I'd stood out on the front road before this house without laying eyes on another living soul. It struck me as odd, but I didn't need an answer. I hadn't spared any love for this brood of people since the day I got off that train, and it seemed the feeling was mutual. I hoisted Alice up onto the horse and said, "Fuck 'em." She had no idea why, I'm sure, but still appreciated the sentiment.

For better or worse, we were off to Lynch's Tavern to confront our destiny. Just had one stop to make first. As it turned out, John Harden was the kind of man to use his birthday to unlock a safe.

We arrived at the outer part of Buzzard's Edge well before the sun climbed overhead.

Alice and I took up a position in a small alley next to Barron's Apothecary. I tied Ghost to a hitch in the narrow, dank alleyway, apologized for the lack of luxury, and removed my hat to peek around the corner. The only people on the other side of the tavern's weather-worn doors would be outlaws and drunks, neither one predisposed to start the day before lunchtime. A dim foreboding lurked in that building, one I should have sensed as soon as evil pulled up a seat in its backroom or cellar.

"Feels like it's watching us," I whispered. "The tavern."

Alice shot me a look I couldn't decipher, but whatever she meant by it didn't inspire confidence.

"Fine, have it your way. I guess we go right in the front. Benefit of me being this thick-headed is I've been sitting on that clue for weeks. They got no reason to suspect today, of all days, is when we find them out and spring."

Alice shrugged. Kid had a point; I was rambling. Some people will always use a bunch of words where one or two would do.

"Okay, okay. What I was gettin' at is, we ought to be okay to go through the front door. I'll kick it in; you stay back. Got your iron?"

A nod of affirmation and she held up the revolver, slightly smaller than the charred one I brought along despite an array of better choices, but still comically large in her hands. All the same, it looked like it belonged there.

I slung a small satchel with extra ammunition and other necessities over my shoulder, then tucked the blackened revolver into my holster, saving that firearm and its lone payload for last. In my right hand, I carried a shiny new pistol, freshly oiled and prepared to spit hell at the two demons inside.

"On three."

No more hesitation now.

"One."

I squeezed the gun's grip so hard, my knuckles blanched of all color.

"Two."

My feet tingled as they prepared for the short sprint and the eventual resistance of the door.

"Three," I whispered.

The door splintered without complaint under the weight of my boot, and I let the momentum carry me inside before I skidded to a stop. My heart shot up into my shoulders, bounced around a bit, then settled on the back of my tongue as I scrambled to find something to grab onto.

Instead of the liquor-stained, piss-smelling floor I anticipated, I came face-to-face with a cliff's edge, dropping off to jagged rocks and a thin, snaking river hundreds of feet below. My toes hovered over the edge as I grabbed onto the door—barely hanging off one hinge—to stop myself going over. Reasonably sure I wasn't about to plunge to my doom, I held up the hand with the pistol and warned the kid back. As a cool breeze drifted up from the bottom of the canyon, I attempted to make sense of this gaping chasm inside a tavern I'd frequented many a time.

A braying laugh drifted across the canyon, and though I couldn't see the source, my blood boiled as I remembered the last time I'd heard it. Before I could think better of it, I fired a round into the open sky in front of me. The laughter cut out, though I didn't believe for a second that I'd hit him. More than that, the sky rippled as though someone shook it like a dirty blanket. The breeze fluttered by again, complete with the sound of running water and something else. A soft whisper, maybe. Confusion settled in as I took in the surreal quality of it all. On a whim, I fired another shot, this time aimed at a promontory rock jutting out from the cliffside. It, too, shimmered when struck, and with the distracting din of Holcomb's laughter gone, returned the sound of glass shattering rather than a bullet ricocheting off rock.

"Shit, kid. I'm about to do something real goddamn stupid. If it doesn't go well, run away."

I sucked in a deep breath, ignored the arguments stemming from the back of my mind, and picked up one foot to let it dangle over the deadly drop. I brought it down, prepared to feel it push through the nothingness and drag me like an anchor to the bottom of that filthy river.

But it didn't.

Despite my theory, I still felt a twinge of surprise when my foot hit solid ground, though nothing supported it besides thin air. That same shimmery movement rippled out from underneath my foot, so vivid it vibrated up through the sole of my boot before overtaking the rest of the landscape and returning it to the familiar setting of the tavern.

The witch.

Whether they somehow knew we were coming or the mirage was a last-minute defense remained a mystery. Either way, hope was elusive. My eyes surveyed the empty room while I dug out two more rounds and refreshed the pistol's cylinder. Shards of glass crunched under my boot, littering the floor beneath a broken mirror. Seeing a building that usually gave home to so much enjoyment and frivolity, but without a single soul inside, created a mighty creepy atmosphere. I almost missed the cliff.

Without turning, I waved the kid in and crept toward the bar, anticipating another illusion or a straight-up gunfight. The floorboards creaked under each step, dispelling any notion that we were sneaking up on shit, yet slow seemed the right choice. I damn near fell over backwards when Lynch popped up from behind the bar like a jack-in-the-box. The tavern's proprietor had stood on the other side of the counter plenty over the years, never smiling, but always ready to provide sustenance. Never once had he pointed a double-barreled rifle at me before now.

"Drop the gun," he said through his trademark scowl. I held his eyes and puffed myself up, trying not to seem too obvious about it. I didn't think he'd seen the kid yet. Then I complied, raising my arms in surrender and allowing the gun to fall to the ground with a discreet clank that sounded too small for the room.

Narrowing my eyes at the traitorous shit, I asked, "Why are you protecting him, Emmett?"

Keeping the rifle trained on me, he let out a low laugh, devoid of humor. "You fucking kiddin', Daggett? This is the closest thing to a future we got. Buzzard's Edge is rotting from the inside out. Maybe it always was. Thing is, Arizona ain't like back east. President Harrison may be in charge, runnin' a land of law and order, but that's not what we got here. Not what we want."

" 'We?' " I asked, careful not to lower my hands. The other revolver weighed at my hip, but any quick motion to retrieve it would find me more porous than I cared for. Besides, that bullet didn't belong to Emmett Lynch.

"Fuck it, then. It's not what I want. Though, there's surely others would rather see the people runnin' this town working together rather than hiding behind a badge, pissing down on the people as they try to carve out a dime."

I gritted my teeth and attempted a calm, level tone. "Harden didn't hide behind a badge. And he certainly never pointed a gun at a kid."

Lynch's glower gave way to confusion and the gun lowered just enough. "Kid? You ain't no kid, Daggett."

Keeping my hands up, I allowed a smirk to sneak onto my face, then stepped to the side. I doubt Emmett Lynch, fuckin' brat that he was, even got a good look at the small human being who put a bullet between his eyes. He crashed backward, taking out a couple shelves' worth of his watered-down liquor. Smoke curled from the end of Alice's pistol. She gripped it tightly in both hands, but her eyes remained cool, promising some grand old tale to be delivered at a later date.

"Goddamn, kid. That was a hell of a shot. Where'd you learn to do that?"

Alice shrugged, then pulled back the hammer and loaded the next shot into the chamber. The breaking bottles had kicked up quite a ruckus, and though Noose and Merella might not know the details, I thought it better to suspect they knew something was wrong. As much as I hadn't liked kicking down the front door without the knowledge of what lay behind it, at least I knew the layout of the main room. After it transformed back from a scenic overlook, that is.

The single door leading to the back of the store held infinite possibilities. Chief among them was Noose Holcomb aiming a six-shooter or two at the closed door, waiting for me to burst through so he could bring this fifteen-year journey to a bloody end. I'd kick it in again, but stay low this time. The plan was less than perfect, but a damn sight better than nothing. Borrowing a page from Alice's book, I waved my hand to shoo her against the wall, out of sight of anyone within the back room, and held up my own pistol to signal she should ready hers.

Before I could think better of it, I crashed my boot into the door and rolled into the room, staying as close to the ground as possible. One revolution and I forced myself to a stop. I pointed the gun around the room, ready to shoot at the first sign of life. Only thing was, this room had a lot more movement than anticipated. I'd tumbled headfirst into a train car, breezing along at top speed. And not just any train car. The train car.

I clambered to my feet, standing in the center of the aisle, surrounded by the grisly scene where he'd left me the first time we met. I recognized the woman who sat across the aisle from me, as well as my dad's suit, though his face was gone. My mother's beautiful turquoise dress, permanently stained with her lifeblood, was the only thing that made her identifiable.

Just an illusion, I told myself, but the witch had recreated the scene exactly as I recalled it. The floor even vibrated under my feet. Had she transported me back in time? I spun around to face the back of the car, noting the guard's body slumped on the floor. Behind his crumpled form, a doorway led back into the tavern. No Alice in sight.

I lifted the revolver and fired it out one of the windows. A small ripple took shape where the bullet met glass, but unlike earlier, the vision held its form. She'd anticipated my clumsy attempts to break the spell. I fired again with the same result, then opted to conserve the rest of the ammunition.

Noose's voice traveled through the train car.

Shoo fly, don't bother me.

Shoo fly, don't bother me.

Shoo fly, don't bother me.

For I belong to somebody.

The verse ended and his voice drifted away following a brief distorted echo, leaving only the sound of the train's engine chugging along and the wheels clacking on the tracks.

"What's a matter, shoo fly? You go on and get too old to sing along with me? Cain't let me start the verse, then leave me all alone to hit the chorus as well. Shee-it, you was raised better than that, wasn't you?"

A tremble overwhelmed my hands at the casual nature of his voice. I was eight years old again, trapped in the grip of a madman, and a slave to his whim. His voice rasped a little bit—even the wicked couldn't run from old age—but it carried the same arrogance I remembered well.

I feel, I feel, I feel like a morning star.

I feel, I feel, I feel like a morning star.

"Say, Rory, think your friend wants to join us for a round?"

"Don't move, Alice." Paralyzed as my body felt, I summoned some lingering preservation for her as well. Noose might kill me here, but he wouldn't make Alice's life what he'd made mine.

"Alice, huh? I wondered about the little urchin's name. You know what happened to her, right? You're smart enough to put that together, ain'tcha?"

"Don't fuckin' tell me you did that to her," I said through clenched teeth. As if I didn't want to separate this asshole's head from his body enough already.

"Me? No. No, no, no," he chuckled. "I'd imagine the only honcho you could hold responsible for whatever's wrong with the girl would be the Lord Almighty hisself. Simply put, if not for her . . ." Noose cleared his throat. "Her infirmity, shall we say, she'd probably be dead as a doornail. See, I sent Edwards to stake out that house and wait in case you came back. Predictable as fuck you were, by the way. He set up shop, but it didn't take him long to figure out he wasn't alone. Quiet as mice that family was, hidin' up in the attic there." A dramatic pause, like he wanted to be sure he had my attention. "It was the baby gave 'em away in the end."

His voice emanated from every direction, flowing in the whistling wind, from the grinding wheels, and pouring in through every window. It originated from every mangled body. Their lips didn't move, but they sang his song anyway. I couldn't see Noose, but his voice contained the hint of a nasty grin. My stomach dropped at hearing how much Alice went through before I'd arrived. All my fault.

"You know how Edwards is with those knives."

"Was," I corrected.

"Right," he said, the smile fading from his tone. "Was. He made quick work of the squatters and prepared the house for the arrival of the prodigal son. Guess he missed a rodent, though."

The doorway still at my back, I raised the gun again and fired, creating a wave at the front of the car on the opposite side of where I'd fired before. I tried to squeeze off another shot, but a thin hiss sounded from behind me and a white-hot heat blasted through the firearm, scalding my palm. I dropped the gun to the floor and shook the agony from my seared hand.

The iron clanked against a wooden floor, despite the thin carpet running down the aisle.

I kept my back to the door and stifled a smile. She'd given herself away. I made no move to retrieve the gun. Instead, I simply stared forward as the satchel's heft tugged at my shoulder.

"Sounds like the girl didn't throw a wrench in your gears none. Don't see why she has to be part of this."

"Well, I don't know 'bout that." The arrogance crept back into his voice. "She shot my landlord just now. Might even have to find a new place to dwell after I deal with your ass. 'Sides, maybe I want her to see the light leave your eyes."

"Alice," I called out. "Get to Ghost, now!" A calculated risk, but one worth taking. I couldn't pinpoint Noose, but I suspected he'd be on the wrong side of the room to catch the girl. I hoped neither him nor the witch could do anything to stop her without disrupting the illusion.

The train chugged along and I heard footsteps fade into the distance. The one squeaky hinge holding the door together gave a dying creak as Alice pushed it aside. I imagined her bursting into the fresh morning air, heading off to keep Ghost company. They'd take care of each other if the next part of the plan didn't work out.

"Now see, shoo fly? I don't care for it all that much when people don't heed my directions. You know that, you done seen it firsthand. So why you wanna go and do a thing like—"

Reaching into my satchel, I wrapped my fingers around the first small piece of glass they stumbled upon. Spinning, I chucked it at the side of the doorway as hard as I could and darted in the opposite direction. Glass exploded and clattered to the hardwood floor. I didn't dare turn to check the color, but the train car illusion gave way to a drab back room.

I crawled to the farthest corner and pulled my shirt over my mouth. Noose, a little grayer but more or less the same man, sat at a table in the opposite corner, unable to mask his shock. A lingering mist of toxic green surrounded Merella as she writhed on the floor. Her dress, composed of deepest midnight black, veiled much of her body, but the skin that showed, bubbled. The fish belly-white of her skin gave way to angry red welts. They grew impossibly fast, then burst like pustules. A scream that promised searing agony accompanied each small explosion upon her skin. Her cries grew louder and more pained for a moment, then diminished, as though she could no longer draw enough breath to convey her pain. She sank to the floor, buried in her heavy cloak while the last of her flesh peeled away, vanishing into nothingness. Only bleached bones remained beneath her shroud.

It was over quickly. No sound or movement came from that side of the room afterward. Even the deadly green chemicals vanished, mixed with the dingy air of the back room and distilled to harmless vapor.

I removed my shirt from my mouth with a trembling hand and took a tentative breath. Merella hadn't died well, and I didn't care to join her. Tearing my eyes from her remains, I turned to Noose, but he wasn't at the table anymore. A sickly old man had replaced him. Thin patches of gray hair dotted his liver-spotted pate and his skin hung sallow off his skeleton. The only things that assured me I was looking at the same man were the shit-eating grin I'd first encountered fifteen years prior and the noose-shaped scar around his neck.

CHAPTER 12

SHOO FLY, DON'T BOTHER ME

His smile widened as he met my gaze, the corners of his lips stretching most of the way to his ears. The grisly sight made it hard not to think of that gaping chasm again. No hat rested upon his head to hide the worn look about him from the world; the stench of grave dirt still bit at my nose.

"Imagine I must look like a pile of shit," he said, studying the back of his thin hands as though they belonged to someone else. Veins protruded like you'd expect on the elderly or infirm. Not the strapping, well-built guy who'd singlehandedly taken over the train car. But that had been fifteen years ago, not fifty.

"Always looked like a pile of shit to me," I mumbled, my tone reverting from the adult who'd kicked in the front door and outwitted a witch back to a scared child. I cleared my throat, willing the fear away.

He folded his hands and rested them on the table. "Have a seat, shoo fly. I ain't gon' shoot you where you stand." It felt like a trick, but I had a revolver and more of Crane's vials, plus the reflexes of a spry twenty-three year old, albeit one who'd had a hell of a couple days.

He let out a sigh as I joined him, deflating as if he were the one taking a load off. "She was the last one, you know."

"I know."

"Yeah, I bet you studied up. All those years. But you didn't catch hide nor hair all that time. Only stories that could've been half bullshit or more."

"I cobbled enough together, but yeah, you 'bout disappeared off the face of the map."

"We went to ground, sure enough. I had high hopes for that train, but son of a bitch, if it didn't exceed every one. And we's a simple folk. Crane didn't want anything so much as time to work on his shit. Disguised himself up every so often to come to town and purchase supplies, but on the level. Merella . . ."

He said the name as though his words could caress. Made me wonder about the nature of their relationship.

"Strange woman," he continued. "Never saw her eat, sleep, or even take a shit. But she was easy enough to entertain and dirt-cheap upkeep. It was Edwards and Dorrance what eventually drove us out of hiding. That big man ate like a fuckin' horse. Probably obliterated half our stores by his lonesome."

"What about Edwards? He wasn't that big." At the back of my mind, a red flag waved furiously, letting me know I'd grown too cozy. Let my guard down.

"Nah, just fuckin' annoying. When I tell you the man had an endless supply of riddles, I bet you'd believe that."

I caught myself nodding and stopped abruptly, saying nothing. A raspy chuckle turned into a cough. "Never would give you the answers if you couldn't guess either. More than once I got to the point where I nearly shoved one of those knives up his ass."

"What about the horse?"

"Been a long time since I thought about him, I guess. Famine. A noble beast that one, but not built to withstand the burden Merella's magic put on him. Buried in the desert more'n twelve years now."

I watched his hands shake, not from fear, but like he couldn't control them anymore. The abrupt change had caught me off guard, but I mostly stared so he wouldn't reach for anything.

"I ain't armed," he said, as if reading my mind. "Not like I'm simple. I got enough guns to slaughter the whole town twice over in the closet there." He was careful to gesture with his head. "Didn't figure you'd get this far, though. Over the years, I put a lot of faith in that woman." This time he nodded to the lump of rags in the corner. I thought I caught a tear dotting the corner of his eye. "Maybe too much. She saved me from hanging, bullets, venom, exposure, starvation, you name it. Saved me from death, in short. I guess I always knew each fix might be temporary, maybe even expected to drop dead right away if'n anything ever happened to her, yet here I am."

There he was, though his pale, waxy skin didn't just tell of age. His heartbeat pounded through the flaps of skin hanging off his scrawny neck, and it raced. At least twice the rate of a normal man. If what he said was true about the guns being out of reach, I could walk out of here and leave him to expire in peace. Only thing that kept me rooted to that seat was a promise I'd made myself nearly every night laying in bed at the Taffs'. A promise that I'd be the one who shuffled George "Noose" Holcomb from this mortal coil.

Unhealthy as the rest of him appeared, his jaundiced eyes kept their animal cunning. He'd already proved himself a competent guesser in regard to what I thought. I figured he probably knew I was too stubborn to walk away now.

"So, Rory—"

Not "shoo fly." Not even "kid." Rory.

"Why me?" The words burst out. "What's so goddamn special about me you couldn't just kill me alongside all the others and be done with it? And why, after all this time, are you still after me?"

He lowered his head to hide a chuckle, but when he raised it, his face was all business.

"You ain't special."

A sputtering cough erupted from his ruined lungs, leaving the words hanging in the air.

"You were there. Simple as that. Just another one of Buzzard's Edge's spoiled rich fuckers, takin' a brand new train for a joyride while the rest of us piddled our lives away in squalor." He left a pause, his scratchy voice betraying his need for a drink. The table remained empty between us. "Stupid me for not anticipatin' a kid aboard. Thinkin' it'd be just the pampered adults, but as soon as I saw you, I knew I couldn't kill you, or let you become one of them."

"A conundrum."

"Precisely. It's like I said back then, Rory. I ain't the worst thing in Buzzard's Edge. I think you knew it then, and I sure as shit believe you know it now."

Tears built at the corners of my eyes, the emotion that drew them slipping into my voice. "Why now? The fuck did I do to you?"

He shot me a hard look, completely devoid of amusement.

"You're tenacious. Didn't think we'd hear about you askin' around for us? We knew what you meant to do, and despite your buddy Harden, you was fixin' to do it outside the law. On more'n one occasion, I thought, 'Golly gee, I could use me one a them on my side.' "

"You killed my parents, Wilhelmina Taff, Harden. Took just about everything I ever had."

He coughed—a wretched rattling sound—then struggled to regain his composure. "I ain't got no use for a man what's tied down. But goddamn, Rory Daggett. Think of all the shit we could accomplish."

I stared at him. Of all the responses floating through my head at the moment, not a single one seemed sufficient, so I simply locked my eyes on his and prayed they breathed the fire I wanted them to.

"What's it to be?" he continued.

In answer, I drew the charred revolver and held it aimed toward the ceiling. "This holster," I said, leading his eyes with mine, "belonged to my father. William Daggett. You shot him without a second thought. Right before you killed my mother. Her name was Mae."

He stared greedily, like a dog waiting for its meal.

I kept my tone level as I could manage, but felt the weight in my chest. Cramming a lifetime's worth of events into the three talismans before me. "The pistol belonged to Mr. Henry Taff. He and his wife gave me a home after the first time you stole everything from me. He was the finest man I ever knew, and the reason I'm gonna give you half a chance to die on your own terms."

Tears crept closer to the edges of my eyes, but I held them at bay through sheer willpower. I opened the cylinder and let a single unused round fall into my hand. "Finally, this bullet. A madman gave it to me the moment after he turned my world upside down."

"You kept it," he whispered. Awe brought a touch of life back into his eyes. He sounded more impressed than nervous.

"I kept it. And I never knew why. Did you expect me to grow up and use it on myself? Save it for you and return the answer one day? I can't ever know, and I don't want you to answer. Because Mr. Holcomb? George? Your days of controlling my life are done. I've killed everyone you know and care about, just for the opportunity to sit across from you and empty this into your skull. But now that I sit here, looking at a pathetic old man, I think I'd rather let you do it." I loaded the bullet back in and pushed the gun across the table. It produced an unsettling scraping sound which echoed through the silent and forgotten back room as loud as a gunshot.

Noose looked at it, but made no move to pick it up. "And . . . and what if I was to pick it up and take a shot at you?"

"You could try." The scared child was gone. "But it'd be the last thing you ever did, and the way your hand is shaking, I don't know that I'd trust my aim if I was you."

He ran a hand over the revolver, gentle, as if petting a small animal. "Guess I always figured you'd want to be the one to pull the trigger." He forced a laugh, but it did nothing to disguise the fear that coursed through his voice, his entire body. "Be able to say you was the one that killed Noose Holcomb." The trembling subsided momentarily, making room for an odd sort of pride that accompanied his name.

I narrowed my eyes at him, bracing my hands against the table to stand up. "Make no fucking mistake, George. I promised myself I'd be the one to kill you. And I have. Whether you pull the trigger or not."

I stood and turned my back on him, then walked across the room. Heat built in the center of my shoulder blades, as I half expected a bullet to cleave through my spine. Although it took less than fifteen steps—I counted every one—the journey was interminable. Thinking of Alice made it easier. The gods had taken enough from me. Some deep down part of me actually believed they'd let me have this one.

When the shot went off, it scared me something awful. My body jerked in anticipation, but when the thump of a corpse collapsing to the floor rang through the room and it wasn't mine, I turned to breathe in the scene. The shot had obliterated any identifiable bits of Holcomb's face. Whoever found him might recognize the scar around his neck and celebrate in the streets, but I doubted they would lament the mess.

Not for a tired old outlaw like him.

The remains appeared almost fake, blotchy skin hanging off a skeleton. But for the mingling aromas of coppery blood, rancid shit, graveyard earth, and something almost like spoiled food—maybe remnants of whatever Merella had done to him—it would be just one more corpse to clean up and throw out back for the circling buzzards to feast upon. Once I turned away, I didn't look back. That part of my life was behind me, and the next phase waited in an alley just outside the front door.

CHAPTER 13

FOR I BELONG TO SOMEBODY

Ghost whinnied, ecstatic, as Alice ran her lithe fingers through the horse's mane. Her current owner had left her in a strange sitting room for days on end and fed her an insufficient amount of oats. Sure, a horse is a horse, but the smart ones know how to gloat.

Ghost looked none-too-pleased when Alice stopped and turned her attention to me. She didn't look surprised to see me alive, but her eyes begged for more information. One piece in particular.

"It's over," I confirmed. Raising a single eyebrow, I asked, "You hear everything he said in there? Even from the other room?"

Alice nodded once, quick and small, and the slight quiver of her lip told me she knew exactly what I meant.

"And that was all true? Baby too?"

Another nod and when the lip trembled to its breaking point, I knew I'd pushed far enough. I lowered a hand to her shoulder.

"Jesus, kid. I'm so sorry," I whispered, and one of the tears that had taken up residence slipped out, dancing down my cheek. "You're with me now. Us orphans got to stick together."

Alice turned her head away so I couldn't see her eyes any longer, but gave a final nod before we hopped on Ghost's back and traveled to Daggett Manor at a leisurely trot. Not a care in the world and no timetable to keep. We knew true freedom in that moment.

A few days passed as we settled into the house, her upstairs and me in the sitting room. It was an odd feeling, dwelling there without the constant need to check over my shoulder. Still, it didn't feel like home. Though it didn't stop Alice, I couldn't go upstairs, knowing Edwards had slaughtered her family, maybe even buried them out back. I guess planting him next to his victims held some kind of justice. I just didn't know which kind that was.

Even though no impending danger cast a pall over those days, I kept expecting somebody to show up looking for Sheriff Harden. Only they never did. The people here didn't give a shit about the man charged with protecting them until they needed that protection again. Then they'd care plenty. The general malaise made it a real challenge to disagree with Noose's final sentiment regarding the people who populated this part of Buzzard's Edge.

The place made me unhappy, and though Alice never complained, I knew it didn't do much for her well-being either. Nevermind Ghost, whose options were limited to the back garden, with its overabundance of corpses, or the sitting room. Simply put, we were three of a kind, and not a one of us belonged in a place like this.

Early one morning—a Tuesday, I think—I woke up with the sun and started gathering items. Clothes, a couple weapons, the leftover vials of Crane's concoctions, and the remaining food from McGregor's. Then I piled it up next to the front door before Alice had a chance to greet the day. When she awoke and saw the pile, I think she knew what I intended, even if the particulars were fuzzy.

The last order of business before we set out was saying goodbye to a friend. I didn't have much to add to the improvised eulogy I gave Harden after burying him, but I did my best to drum up something kind. Alice remained by the back door, head bowed, maybe saying goodbye to her family, maybe offering me a bit of privacy. I didn't ask.

Boarding up the windows before our departure crossed my mind, but I had no desire to touch that hammer again. Besides, if someone wanted to squat there, they'd be putting the house to better use than abandon and inevitable rot. A couple more trips back and I might even stop locking the door. William and Mae Daggett worked hard for this life, but it wasn't mine. Truth be known, I'm not sure what they would have thought of that, being deprived of their company most of my life. I like to believe they would have understood.

No, I craved simplicity, and I knew just where to get it.

The remains of Taff Ranch didn't offer any more promise under the light of this new day, but I held fast hope anyway.

Ghost's pace picked up a little as she approached the outskirts of Buzzard's Edge and took in the familiar landscape. If Alice had any reaction to the place we'd be hanging our hats, she didn't show it.

The barns and stables stood right as rain, and although the animals looked plump, Tom Corley hadn't got around to moving them to his place just yet. Maybe he'd even let them stay. Tom always had been a friendly bastard, and I guessed I wouldn't mind having him as a neighbor.

It wasn't perfect, but the barn would provide a roof over our heads while we got to work. The coming days would hold a hell of a lot of clean up and the hardest work my hands ever experienced. Alice's too. But I knew we were up for it. When the new house was finished, it would look miles different than the old one. It had to. Because even though my heart still held all the love in the free world for the Daggetts and for the Taffs, I had to make it my own. We had to make it our own.

And that was alright.

AFTERWORD

Noose was my first real attempt at a western story. I'd dabbled with tropes of the genre incorporated into a fantasy setting, but I wanted to create something that took place in lawless land of the 1800s American west, albeit with some supernatural elements. I do fancy myself a horror writer, after all.

There were a lot of research breaks in the writing and a lot more during the editing. I like to think I got enough right to drag you in and if I got anything wrong, the characters kept you turning the pages. Rory and Alice are both special to me and I would be shocked if I don't pick up with them in the not-too-distant future. But Noose. Oh man, George Holcomb. Such a bastard and yet so much fun to write. I played with the kind of relationship a man like him might have with a witch, and though I kept it surface-level in the novella you just read, it stayed in the back of my mind for about six months until I finally decided I had to write it.

So turn the page and check out "Come and Take My Hand", a coming-of-age quasi-prequel where you, the reader, get a chance to come along as I dig under the skin to see who George Holcomb and Merella really are and how they came to be where we met them in Noose.

If you enjoy this little look at the Buzzard's Edge universe, there are two more stories coming your way in the fall of 2022. "Trade Secrets" is my attempt at a Sherlock Holmes-ian detective dropped in the middle of the Arizona desert. It's a whodunit that heavily features Sheriff John Harden from

Noose and a new character, Thaddeus Locke, who may have some more stories to tell in the future. Eagle-eyed readers may notice that Harden "might know a guy" who can help them round up Noose's gang. This story will appear in Blood in the Soil, Terror on the Wind, edited by Kenneth W. Cain and put out by Brigids Gate Press.

"Holes" will appear in Hot Iron and Cold Blood: An Anthology of the Weird West, edited by Patrick R. McDonough and published by Death's Head Press. "Holes" was originally written for a splatterpunk anthology and it shows, a little more in your face than some of the other Noose-iverse stories. It features no characters from the book, but ties into some of the events that take place therein. My story aside, this anthology features Joe R. Lansdale, Edward Lee, Kenzie Jennings, Ronald Kelly, Briana Morgan, Owl Goingback, David J Schow, and more.

Before I let you go, I may have holed up in my back office to write this book, but there's a lot of people who helped it get to its present state. Huge thanks to Erica Robyn and Patrick McDonough, two of the world's best humans, for reading an early version and providing invaluable notes. Elford Alley graciously read "Come and Take My Hand" to see if it could truly stand alone, and I thank him for his feedback.

My wife, Aron, continues to give me the time and freedom to bang away at this keyboard when I could be out getting a real job (a third one), and I love her dearly for it. My boys, Dallas and Dustin, don't give me the time, but are usually in bed by eight. Writing is dependent on life experience, and without them, I'd be missing an awful lot of that.

Andrew and the entire family, yep family, at Dark Lit Press has been phenomenal to work with. I can't thank him loud enough for taking a chance on this book. Once again, Donnie

Goodman took a partially formed cover idea and made magic with it. Kristina at Truborn Design ran with that and made the book an exterior to be proud of.

To Lee Murray, Alan Baxter, and Tyler Jones, who were gracious enough to read early copies and provide some kind words. Thank you to everyone in this horror genre who reads and reviews. Your work is underappreciated but vital. Without it, my work fizzles away into nothingness.

A special thank you to Ronald Kelly and Tyler Jones, who offer a constant conversation on writing. Both of you have made me better at this than I have any right to be. There's a long road ahead, but I'm honored to be driving by your side.

THE END?

WAIT! THERE'S MORE...

COME

AND TAKE

MY HAND

Brennan LaFaro

"Time for bed, Georgie." Janie Holcomb leaned on the kitchen table and inclined her head toward the boy's bedroom. "Got to be up with the sun tomorrow and you ain't sleep well last night."

George blinked as if the action could hide the dark circles beneath his eyes. "I couldn't sleep, Mama."

"And why ever not?" Janie crossed her arms and fixed her gaze deeper than George's eyes. He got the feeling she could study the back of his skull if she so desired.

George shifted his foot, scraping it against the rough floorboard.

"Out with it."

"She's watchin', Mama. That woman I told you 'bout."

Janie lowered her head, eyes squinted and nostrils flared. A moment passed.

"It's true!" George stared down at his feet. "It's like the night gets darker, she sucks up the moon and stars, and then she looks in. Never tries the latch or nothin'. Just…watches, and—.""

Janie sighed. "Is that all? George Holcomb, you're too old for such fairy tales to be occupyin' the space between your ears."

"But Mama, she—"

"I won't hear another word about it." Her tone softened and the barest hint of a smile shone through, just enough to display a tooth-sized gap. "You'll be alright, Georgie. Had a bad dream is all. Now get your behind to bed 'fore your father gets home and…" She shook her head and her smile dropped away. A shiver rippled through her shoulders.

It ain't even cold in here, thought George.

"You listen to your Mama now." Any trace of anger had deserted her voice. "Go on."

The tiny hairs stood on the back of George's neck as he peeked past the kitchen and into his room. A pulse rippled through the shadows, beckoning. He curled his toes, scraping them against the unforgiving floor. Whatever awaited him paled in comparison to his mother's ire and father's belt. Without a word, he turned and scuttled off toward his room, his mother's stare drilling into the space between his shoulder blades as if in search of oil.

Averting his eyes from the window, George changed clothes in a hurry and threw himself into the bed. Candlelight flickered in from the kitchen, lending motion to the already dizzying array of shadows. He pulled the covers up over his head, breathing fast and hard in the enclosed space. The slight orange glow permeated the thin sheet. At least Mama was still awake and watching over him. When the candle's light orange hue cut off suddenly, his heart took off like a jackrabbit.

Footsteps approached.

"No wonder you're scared of the dark, blanket pulled up over your head and all. Come outta there, Georgie. Let me see that face one more time tonight." Mama's comforting weight settled next to him on the bed.

Reluctantly, George lowered the blanket. "You ever get scared, Mama?"

"All the time, but gettin' older means facing your fears instead of hidin' from 'em." She looked down at her lap. "Of course, facing fears can mean all kinds of things, can't it?"

George lowered his voice to a conspiratorial whisper. "What scares you most?"

"Truth?"

"Of course."

"Something happenin' to you. Sometimes being grown up means meeting your fears head on, but sometimes it means doing everything you can, and that ain't always pleasant, to keep the monsters away from those you love. Know what I mean?"

George nodded, though he wasn't sure he understood.

"If you don't now, you will someday in the future. I'll make sure of it." She stood with a sigh and crossed the room. "Sleep tight, sweet thing." Mama's words floated across the room, soothing the discomfort that hung in the air. As she left his doorway, the candle light danced for a moment longer before Janie Holcomb extinguished it. With George put to bed, she'd likely grown tired of waiting for her husband to lumber in from the tavern. Sometimes Father didn't crash through the front door until nearly sunup, but he always came home.

Still hidden beneath the safety of the covers, George's heart slowed to a normal pace. His breathing became deep and steady, peaceful. Sleep lurked at the edges of his vision with outstretched fingers, waiting to take him.

Skreeeeeeeeeeeeek.

Something scratched at his windowpane. Beads of sweat gathered on George's forehead, threatening to fall. He clutched the sheet so tight that his fingernails dug through the thin linen and bit into his palms.

George wanted to stay wrapped in its comforting warmth, but he knew who raked at the window. Time and panic would transform her face into something more terrible than reality. In his imagination, her teeth descended into glistening fangs, eyes yellowed, taking on the vertical slit pupil of a goat, and her already pallid skin dimmed to resemble a chalky white found only in death.

A fairy tale, Mama had said. Just a fairy tale. George gritted his teeth and tossed the blankets off. They landed on the wood floor with a soft clump. It was the only sound in the house. He scrunched his eyes shut but the darkness surrounded him still.

Skreeeeeek.

Shorter and a little softer this time. More like a gentle caress than a threatening note. But still, she waited. Not a fairy tale.

Raising one eyelid at a time, George turned his attention to the window. There she was. The woman in the window, draped in fabric so black she was almost lost against the night.

Woman.

George shook his head as though he'd spoken the thought aloud. That wasn't right. She couldn't have been much older than his eleven years. Her skin glowed soft and white, but it told of life rather than death. The girl's light blue eyes gleamed with sadness, maybe longing. Her pursed lips curved into the ghost of a smile, and relief flowed through him. Those lips were not large enough to hide the imaginary pointed teeth that had filled him with dread only moments ago.

She lifted a hand to the window and pressed her fingertips against the glass. No shrieking scratch this time, only a barely audible tap. The five fingers hung before George, begging his understanding. George's feet carried him across the room without permission, drawn by her icy blue eyes. She never stayed this long the other nights. Always disappeared as if lured away by the light of the moon before he could decide what to do.

Always leaving him wondering if it was a dream or not.

Not this time.

With only thin glass separating them, the girl lowered her hand and stepped back, waiting expectantly. Open the window, said something in George's mind. Just a crack will do.

He obeyed.

The sweet and spicy aroma of cinnamon drifted into the room. George offered a shy smile. "Gets awfully cold out here at night. Don't you got no place to sleep?" Before she could answer, he continued, "Mama says all them critters what love the hot sand are ascared of the cold, so you ain't got to worry 'bout rattlers or scorpions when the moon takes over the sky. That why you're out here at this time of night?"

The edges of her smile lifted. When she spoke, her voice was flat and lacked the emotion that lived in her eyes. "Something like that. I prefer to walk at night, avoid the sun, the critters, and the...people."

George cocked his head. "If you're looking to avoid people, coming up and tappin' on a window sure is a strange way to go about it."

"Something always catches my attention when I walk by your house, George. By your window. It's hard to describe, but I guess the best way to put it is...a light."

"Mama usually leaves a candle lit until she gives up and goes to bed, tired of waitin' for my——-" George raised his eyebrows. "Say, I don't believe I gave out my name."

"I know."

"Well, seems only fair I should know yours then." He smiled, allowing any lingering nerves to drip away.

"Merella," she said.

"Well, Merella, that's a lovely na——"

Crash.

From the other side of the house, the front door had burst open and clattered against the wall. George's heart climbed up his throat and tried to get a grip on the back of his tongue before it plunged down and plopped into his stomach.

"That's my daddy," George whispered. "He'll be crosser'n a snakebit horse he comes in and sees you. Best you move along."

Merella nodded and George reached to close the window, but hesitated. Footsteps stomped across the kitchen floor.

"Wouldn't upset me none if you knocked on my window tomorrow night, though." He flashed a sheepish grin.

"Maybe I will," Merella whispered. Then she vanished as if a hole had materialized in the night air and swallowed her.

George eased the window shut and tiptoed back to bed, pulling the covers up a second before the hulking frame of his father filled the doorway. The scant moonlight glinted off the man's belt buckle, but the rest of him remained enveloped by shadow. Squeezing his eyes shut and attempting to mimic the steady breathing that came with sleep, George said a silent prayer that his father would bypass his room that night. The stink of sweat and grain alcohol filled his nose, relegating the smell of cinnamon to a distant memory. It sent his heart racing even as he felt the piercing gaze on him. After what seemed like hours, the statue in the doorway let out a rumbling belch and stumbled away.

Before long, the familiar babble of muffled pleas, thwacks of leather against flesh, slapping of skin on skin, and animalistic rutting came from the other room. George recited another prayer for his mother, figuring if the first one had worked, maybe the second one might stand a chance.

"Rise n' shine, Georgie."
Janie Holcomb shook George awake before the first beam of Arizona sunshine poured in the window. He wrestled his eyes open, knowing the morning light would peer over the horizon any second.
When it did, he caught a glance of dried blood at the corner of her lip. Only a speck, but it drew his eyes like flies to a horse's behind. Janie wiped at her face, banishing the bloody spot to oblivion.
"Mama."

"Ne'er you mind, Georgie. Get your lazy backside out of bed and go help your father." She raised her eyebrows, but George missed whatever she might be trying to communicate with the gesture. "Don't want to keep 'im waitin'," she whispered.

George dressed quick as a startled bird and dashed outside. His morning chores had changed not a whit in years, yet his father still delighted in supervising as though the boy was too damn stupid to keep a thought in his head. Feeding the pigs was always the first order of the day, as they made the most godawful noises when forced to wait. Let the pigs go hungry a mite too long and the entire animal population falls into upheaval. Easing toward the sty, George kept an eye out for his father, who mainly kept to the shadows, popping out when George least expected it.

The wet slap of pig slop pouring into the trough covered the sound of his father's approach, but George's heart skipped a beat at the aroma of the pungent tobacco that always accompanied the man in the morning. The pigs went to work, their only job to gorge themselves and make for a tastier and more plentiful meal one day. George watched them, wondering if they'd eat his father as greedily as they devoured that slop.

"Glad to see you up with the sun, boy." Father's voice resembled an odd mixture of a grumble and a croak. "Your mama said you was havin' nightmares or some such bullshit."

"Yes, sir," said George. Putting aside last night's encounter, nightmares wasn't the right word, but any other answer might start a conversation George didn't particularly care to have.

A light rustle drifted down as his father sucked on the hand-rolled cigarette. "Too old to be havin' nightmares, you ask me. And surely too fuckin' old to be cryin' to your mama about it."

"Yes, sir." George gripped the wooden fence so hard his knuckles turned white. He fought the urge to spin around and glimpse the smirk his father undoubtedly wore. An exaggerated exhale filled the air around him with bitter smoke. A test. George held his breath to stifle any rogue coughing fits. "A man what seen real horrors might revisit those things in his dreams every so often. But he learns to get up every mornin' and bury all that shit. Ain't no son a mine gon' be pissin' in his pants over a boogeyman. Hear me, boy?"

George squeezed the fence so tightly he half-expected to find fingerprints embedded in the wood later on. How much more pressure would he need if this were his father's throat and not some lifeless hunk of lumber?

"Yes, sir."

"God damn right."

The embers of the cigarette crackled softly as father took another hefty draw, then dropped it to the ground and stomped on it. A metallic clink made George's heart race and the whooshing scrape of a leather belt pulled free from its confines confirmed his worst fears.

George squeezed his eyes shut, uttering a silent prayer for the leather strap and not the buckle this time. Surely nightmares didn't make for a bad enough transgression to merit the jagged metal wielded by his father like a medieval weapon. He held his breath, tensed his muscles, and waited for the first blow.

A joyless chuckle crept out of Father's mouth. This was all part of a cruel waiting game to drain fear from George before exacting the desired pound of flesh.

Bracing himself against the fence, George gritted his teeth and rocked back and forth, anticipating the harsh sting, almost craving the pain, just to get it done with. He would take his lashes and let his tears fall and then forget the shame when Merella knocked at his window that night. He opened his eyes at the thought of the lovely girl. The faint scent of cinnamon washed away the lingering odor of cigarette smoke. As if the very thought of her cleared his senses, George relinquished his grip on the fence and looked around in confusion.

He was alone.

If Janie Holcomb thought it odd that her little Georgie went from piss-your-pants scared of the woman at the window to accepting over the course of a day, she said nothing. Perhaps she suspected he'd been convinced to drop it. And with good reason. It wasn't often that George's father removed his belt and failed to employ it.

George watched her go about her tasks, stopping every so often and wincing as she rubbed her right shoulder. When she returned to her work, she favored the left hand a bit more than usual. George understood the cause, but kept his mouth shut. The aftermath of discipline wasn't something they ever talked about, but seeing Mama like that only stoked fire in George's belly. For now, he had it under control, but too much fuel and it threatened to escape its confines and set the world aflame.

The sunlight hours passed in a flash and George went to bed without a fuss. Maybe a little too early, because the kitchen candle shared its warm light for quite some time before Mama finally put it out. Merella said that light drew her to George's window, but he didn't think she'd come to call with those flames flickering.

Darkness closed in, but George kept it at bay with hope. At first, anyway. The more time that passed without a gentle rap at the window, the deeper his heart sank. When it finally came, George sprung from the bed and nearly flew across the room.

Merella greeted him with a subdued smile and shining eyes, then backed away so he could open the window.

George expected the window to creak, but it held its tongue. Clumsy as he was, he feared tumbling out the window and making a racket that would bring Mama running. Even if he escaped all that unscathed, Merella and he would undoubtedly run headlong into George's father, soused as the night is long, and nursing a mean streak wider than the Grand Canyon.

"Come and take my hand," she said, as he raised a leg to step out the window.

Butterflies fluttered in George's guts as he walked side-by-side, hand-in-hand, with Merella. Sweat coated his palm, while hers remained dry and cool as the Arizona night. She seemed perfectly content to travel in silence, their footsteps scraping sand was the only accompaniment. After rejecting a bevy of opening lines, George settled on one.

"Where do you live?"

"I've lived all over. For the moment, here in Buzzard's Edge." George's heart plummeted. "Where in town, I mean?" he asked, crossing his fingers it was somewhere nearby. He didn't think he could bear hearing her home lay in the center of the city, where the rich snobs would never let their lovely daughters mingle with an outskirter like him.

"If I told you that, George, what would you do? Walk me home?"

"I s'pose not. Just curious, is all. Don't your parents worry 'bout you?"

She smiled. "Don't yours?"

"Well, I don't suspect they know I'm out. Otherwise, I'd be in for a whuppin'." He forced a laugh, but Merella only narrowed her eyes.

"Sometimes I see your mother through the window. She looks kind. Tired, but gentle. I never see your daddy."

George stiffened, felt his chest go tight. It wasn't a question, but he still felt inclined to answer.

"Good."

Merella showed no trace of surprise. "Why?"

"He's just…" He studied Merella's eyes, hoping they'd tell him the follow-up was only her being polite, but curiosity lived in them. He sighed, then whispered, "He ain't good to us. Wouldn't be right to say much more than that."

Merella didn't answer. Instead, she studied George's face. A cold prickle climbed the back of his spine and he suspected she saw everything. Feared she actually saw everything.

When she broke her gaze, she said nothing, but placed her free hand over her lips and turned away. He followed her in silence, pulled in the direction of the still and unbroken horizon. George's eyes darted back and forth between Merella and the ground. He'd seen the girl disappear into nothingness the previous night and didn't plan on losing her ever again.

Wherever she was taking him, it wasn't her home. They wandered into the desert, past small sprigs of plantlife, riddled with thorns and hardy enough to survive the harsh daylight hours. The vermin had bedded down for the night and only the moon overhead accompanied them, until they came to a lonely foothills palo verde tree, its branches stretched toward the sky in defiance of the unforgiving elements. A plume of life in the otherwise barren landscape. Merella donned a pleased smile, and sat at its base, patting the ground next to her. George filled the spot.

"What do you think?" she asked.

The sand stretched endlessly in every direction, swallowed by the darkness at the edge of the moon's limits. George squinted in the direction of town, trying to make out the shadow of buildings.

"S'gorgeous," he said, turning his eyes back to her. "Uh, you come out here often?"

"When I can. People tend to avoid this place, but that's because they don't know what the dawn brings."

George paled and Merella laughed, a light and lovely sound. "Don't worry. We don't have to stay out until morning. Just a hint of sun and you'll see. We're at the perfect point, halfway between the town and the mountains. It feels like you're holding the two at bay, and yet, neither one can ever touch you."

The lovely words Merella strung together reminded him of Mama reading poetry aloud. An attempt to find beauty in the desolate landscape of their lives. George never could grasp what the poets were getting at, but knew there was something bigger at play than the words themselves.

George's heartbeat sped up again as Merella wrapped her cool, white fingers around his own. Colder than the night air and whiter than milk.

"What do you want to be, George Holcomb?"

His throat went dry and his mind blank. "A farmer," he said, the first answer that sprang to his mind. Then he shook his head.

"Think about it. Don't answer too quickly."

A moment passed, then another. George imagined the moon ferrying across the night sky, ticking away his time with this mysterious girl. Then the answer came to him.

"Free." Despite Merella's instruction, the word passed George's lips before his mind could wrench it back.

"Free," she repeated, almost tasting the word. "Are you not free now?"

His face reddened and he hoped Merella hadn't noticed. He could only shake his head in reply.

She studied him. "Your Daddy?"

George shifted uncomfortably. "Mama always taught me not to call him Daddy, but to call him Father. Even that might be too generous."

"What is he then?"

"A monster." His eyes wandered the coarse desert floor for a moment, then he raised them again. "Don't mean to be rude, but can we talk about something else?"

Merella shrugged. "Change nothing and nothing changes."

George nodded but said nothing for fear of slipping back into the same conversation.

"There," she said.

As if on cue, the vague, almost illustrated outline, of Buzzard's Edge came starkly into view. Only with the shadowed buildings scattered like a child's toy blocks, did George realize how far they'd traveled. To the right and left, the land stretched toward an inevitable horizon. George had never seen the ocean, but had heard stories about it and it seemed just as endless as this sandy sea. At their backs, the suggestion of sunlight peeked between the jagged tips of the Blackjack Mountains. They were titans, black shadows that loomed over George's world, they promised adventure and made his heart soar.

Merella saw only him. She conjured a coy smile. "I told you."

"Hot damn," he said, just above a whisper, the loudest volume he could summon.

"It never gets any less—"

She stopped suddenly, the smile drifting away from her lips and her eyes squinting as she jerked her head around.

George heard it too. Buzzing, almost like an approaching swarm of locusts. Sweat gathered on his brow and his stomach lurched. His mind barely had time to place the all-too-familiar alarm before two points of white heat sank into the back of his hand.

That wasn't buzzing.

A greenish-brown serpent pumped its venom into George's veins. The rattling intensified, emanating from a white-ringed tail that shook so violently, it became a blur. Its task complete, the snake relinquished its grip then shot across the sand as if the vengeful Old Testament God were hot on its trail. It vanished in the shadow of the mountains.

"Oh shit, oh shit, oh shit!" yelled George, holding onto his right wrist with his left hand. "It's swellin' up already. Don't it look bigger?"

Merella's gaze followed the snake, resting on the mountains and the dawn's light rising over their peaks.

"We have to get back. Maybe Doc Harrison can do somethin' but we gotta go!" Merella did not budge. "You listenin'?"

"It's too far," she said, absently. "That was a Mojave green, the worst one around here. White bands on the tail." She turned to meet his eyes with tears dancing at the edge of her own. "I'm sorry," she said.

"You're sorry?" he squeaked. George's eyes opened impossibly wide, and his breath came in short, desperate pants. "You mean—" He sucked in a wheezy breath. "I'm just goin' to have to die. That's all?"

She shook her head. "I didn't want to…" Merella left the sentence unfinished and huffed in impatience. "Take my hand."

George had not hesitated when Merella made the offer through the window and in spite of his panic, he accepted once more. She gripped his swollen hand firmly, causing him to grimace.

Her free hand sprang to life, not unlike the fleeing rattler, waving pale fingers in a boneless manner. Her intense gaze contained fire as her hand danced gracefully through the air. Tingles filled his inflamed hand, followed by a searing heat. The invisible fire caused more pain than Father had ever inflicted. George tried to jerk his hand away, but it remained locked in her grip. A ferocity took over her soft facial features and he questioned if he ever should have trusted her in the first place.

Merella's movements became more frantic, rapid and unpredictable. Tracers followed the swirling movement of her hand. Sweat trickled down the sides of her temples and George found himself paying more attention to her face than his hand. The sweet fragrance of cinnamon lingered in the air and the agony, now spread throughout his body, bordered on unbearable.

With a final burst of wriggling, Merella thrust her hand skyward and a flurry of amber liquid erupted from George's bulging hand. The yellow globules hung in the air just above their heads, maybe two dozen in all, glimmering under the first rays of the morning sunlight.

The venom, thought George.

The tiny pockets of liquid floated lazily as George watched. Perhaps more stunning than the view of the mountains. With a flick of her wrist, Merella conducted the bubbles like a symphony, as if picking particular notes from the air. The liquid danced in the morning air, certain death transformed into something dazzling and lively. With the song at its end, she whisked her free hand into the air and the venom careened into the sky, gone in a heartbeat.

"What are you?" George whispered, wincing at his indelicate phrasing.

Merella yanked her hand free and covered her face. Light sobbing sounds emanated from within. "Please don't ask it like that."

"I don't mean no harm by it. I…I think you're amazing."

"The hell you do. You think I'm a monster. You'll tell everyone and I'll have to find another home. Don't you lie to me, George. It'll only make all this harder."

"Hey now," said George. "I wouldn't lie to you. I don't think you're a monster, Miss Merella. Why, I think you might be just about the most beautiful piece of work God ever done put on this earth." A moment passed. "And I won't tell a soul what I saw."

A single bloodshot eye peeked from between her fingers.

"I mean it," he added.

"I see that."

"I hate to be so brisk, but that sun's peepin' over the horizon and I'm already goin' to catch hell, but if we hurry back, I might catch a little less." He smiled as if joking, though they both recognized the truth of the statement.

"Okay," she said, dropping her hands. "Okay. But is it alright if maybe we don't talk about what just happened?"

"Course. One condition, though. Will you come and visit me again tomorrow? Maybe we don't run so far away this time," he said, holding up his right hand, good as new, "but, I sure would like to see you."

"I'd like that, George. Count on it."

George and Merella ambled across the packed sand, conversing in stolen glances and flickering smiles that said everything.

George hauled himself up to the window. As he lowered in silently, he turned to steal one more glance at Merella, but she was gone.

Magic, that one.

A throat cleared from the shadowy corner of his room and the stupid grin dropped from George's face. He hadn't thought to avoid trouble completely, but he hoped he'd get closer than this.

A twirl of smoke wandered into the light, trailing from one of his father's stinky hand-rolled cigarettes. The acrid smoke and the stench of whiskey overtook the room. George wondered how he'd missed it upon opening the window.

Like the devil himself hid that scent.

If he'd caught a whiff, he might have slammed the window shut and run off for better prospects. Hell, he'd take the snakes in those mountains over this. Then again, he knew he'd never leave Mama alone to deal with Father. Not much he could do now, but one day he knew he'd be big and mean enough to challenge his father.

That day wasn't today, though.

The curling smoke framed the gargantuan figure still hidden in shadow.

"Where was you, boy?"

George's head filled with buzzing—no, rattling, a muffled version of the rattlesnake's sudden warning.

"I'll say it again," said the gruff voice. "I been sittin' here for more'n a few hours and that bed's remained empty as the Lord's tomb on Easter Sunday. So, where the fuck you been?"

George remained silent, well aware the wrong words might change the severity of the discipline.

A low chuckle sounded, reminding George of boots stomping down a flight of stairs. When the laughter trailed off, a metallic snikt floated from the dark side of the room. Goosebumps rose on the back of George's neck at the familiar sound, and his blood turned to ice. The silhouette remained still, but George understood what his father was preparing for.

"You won't tell me straight out, I'll get it out of you the best way I know how. One thing sure as Hell. You ain't gettin' out that window no more."

My God, what a world you love, George thought.

"Drop trou, boy, and get ready to repent."

That night, Janie Holcomb blew out the candle with a soft whoosh.

"Sleep tight, sweet thing," she said, but embarrassment crept into her voice.

Her light footsteps trailed off toward the kitchen, abandoning George to the pitch dark of his bedroom. Three muffled taps pecked at the windowpane. George balled his fists, wrapping them in the covers. Each tap sent a shiver up his spine. What was the point of walking over to her? George wasn't strong enough to pry loose the newly-installed boards that covered his window.

Tap-tap-tap!

More urgent now.

He squeezed his eyes shut, wishing Merella would just pass by. Find another window.

"George?" She spoke softly, but the wood and glass didn't muffle the sound. He opened his eyes wide, coming face to face with the beautiful girl, only inches from his bed. Her sweet scent filled the room. He pulled the covers over his head.

"Did I do something wrong?"

George held his tongue, but trembled.

"No. God, no. Merella…" he started, but needed to say no more. He dragged himself out from under the covers.

A gentle light glowed in the palm of her hand. Not enough to draw attention from elsewhere in the house, but sufficient to illuminate the wide-eyed look of horror on her face. She covered her mouth with her free hand.

"What has he done to you?" she whispered.

George forced a smile, but dropped it when he realized Merella didn't buy the false bravado. "Nothin' he ain't done a hundred times before. How…How are you doing that?" he asked, inclining his head toward the light sheathed within her hand.

She ignored the question and cradled George's bruised cheeks, staring into his blackened eyes as though she might find a deeper answer there. He had none to give.

"Don't s'pose you could fix me up again?" he asked.

She shook her head. "There's a sizable chasm between fear and hate. One I'm not yet sure how to cross. Hate leaves deeper scars."

George nodded, though he did not understand. He began to get out of bed, winced as his backside lit up in agony, and then pushed through to stand next to her. George stood bow-legged as if having spent the day atop a mustang. When he opened his eyes from their squinting position, Merella's expression startled him.

Her eyes bugged from their sockets and her lips moved soundlessly. Somehow, she became paler. Although she looked at George, she appeared to stare through him and into the dark recesses of the unlit kitchen. A surge of adrenaline raced through his body as it went rigid, but the doorway remained empty.

"He won't ever let you grow," she whispered. "He'll kill you first."

"No." George studied his bare toes, unable to meet her gaze when he said it. "I mean, he lets me have it, sure enough, but deep down he cares for me. For Mama." The longer George spoke, the less he believed his own words, and Merella appeared no more convinced than himself.

"It might be an accident, or at least look like one, but make no mistake, he will kill you." She eyed the dried crimson stain along his sheets. "George! No one who professes to love you would do such a thing." The shockingly stern tone demanded his attention. He looked up, saw the pain in her eyes.

A dark feeling rose inside George, bringing a bout of nausea with it. Truth, he thought. He'd always believed his father to be a good man, if a little detached, who got carried away when administering discipline.

Merella reached for his hand. "You said it yourself, he's a monster."

George took her hand and nodded slowly.

"And monsters don't stop being monsters if given time and enough slack on their lead. Monsters must be vanquished, or they will go on hurting, perhaps killing, indefinitely."

Tears gathered at the corners of George's eyes. "Can you stop him?"

The steel in her eyes subsided.

"You walked right through the dang wall in my bedroom. Course you can!" pleaded George. "You saved my life from that rattler. That was a monster, too."

"That snake was scared. It struck out of fear because we were in its home. Monsters seek trouble. They don't flee like a scared serpent."

"So what? What's the difference?"

"My power has limits. Boundaries, if you like. You'll need to be the one to fight your father."

"But...but I'm scared."

"There is no power I can summon quite as strong as one who has been wronged. One who seeks revenge."

"He's bigger'n me, though."

"And he knows it. Use that to your advantage. I can't fight him for you, George. But I can help."

He sat back on his bed, grimacing as his battered ass hit the mattress. "I'm listening."

"I'll need to think on it." She smirked. "I'm afraid I wasn't expecting this. It's not like I had a battle plan drawn up."

"Nah, I get it," said George. "You need to go to that tree, and sit a spell, I'll be alright here. Even if I could get out the house, I don't think I could hobble all the way there."

She stared at him for a moment as though he'd asked a question. "Can I show you something, George?"

"Of course." His heart fluttered.

"And you promise not to be scared?"

"Hell, I promise to try."

She pulled her hand away and closed her eyes, then began moving her hands through the air the way she had done to heal George earlier. Faster and faster until her fingers seemed to multiply in a frantic blur. The hardwood floor shifted to a lighter hue. The cracks between slats vanished as the knots in the wood swirled to become whirlpools of sand.

George's eyes wandered the room. The ceiling gave way to a star-filled night sky and the walls vanished, leaving behind only open air. The shadows that perpetually lived in George's room took on the shapes of the Blackjack Mountains. The cool night air brushed against his cheeks and he knew if he shifted his gaze ever so slightly, he would see Merella's tree, but he only turned enough to see her.

Concentration filled her eyes as she willed the scene into existence. The trace of a smile lit her face as she snuck a peek at George, and the moon became his boarded-up window once more. Her grin faltered and she turned her attention back to the mountains. Her own version of freedom.

George felt the sand between his toes, felt the cold desert breeze ruffle his hair. And then it was gone. The rough wooden floorboards returned beneath his feet and Merella collapsed on his bed, her breathing labored and her hands still.

"Did you really take us out there?" he whispered.

She shook her head. "I can make people see things. Play on emotions. Joy and fear are the easiest to work with."

"Wow."

She interlocked her hands in front of her. "You're not frightened?"

"Not even a little. Merella, I don't think you could ever hurt me."

Worry creased her face, but it was gone in a second. "I have to go."

"But you'll be back tomorrow? And we'll figure all this out?"

She nodded and helped George into bed, then lightly kissed the corner of his mouth. Backing away, she wriggled her fingers and disappeared into the shadows.

For the first time all day, George's backside didn't bother him. He was floating.

George lay awake for hours after Merella left, afraid his father would arrive home, further in his cups than ever and ready to unleash hell. His heavy eyelids betrayed him before long and if his father arrived with his usual ceremonial ruckus, George did not stir at the cacophony.

That morning, George beat the sun to rising. He fixed himself a small breakfast, quiet as possible so as not to wake Mama before her time. A hopeful air helped him push through the razor-sharp pain that jolted through every step as he made his way outside.

The still morning air lacked that low, sludgy voice that reveled in correcting mistakes, real or imagined. George tensed his shoulders, expecting his father to appear around each and every corner.

Maybe it finally happened. Maybe the bastard drank himself to death.

George allowed himself a hint of relief at the thought, but dismissed it just as quickly. It was too easy. When a knight arrived to fight a dragon, he never found the dragon dead in the cave, having choked on a cow bone. No, monsters required slaying. If the world took care of them in the first place, George wouldn't have spent his first eleven years living in fear.

An odor caught George's attention outside the pigsty, freezing him in place. Not just the usual shit stink the pigs gave off in spades, but an accompanying offense that stung the nostrils. Whiskey.

A reek that clung to his father like hair to a tarantula, and it wafted from inside the sty. Darkness claimed the contents within as the rising sun had yet to reach that far.

George inched closer to the dim sty and peered around the corner, fearing one of his father's cruel tricks. The man lay sprawled in a haystack, naked to the waist and surrounded by his own sick. His breeches hung open, revealing a nest of pubic hair strangling his penis.

Bile rose in George's throat and for a moment, he thought the man might be dead after all.

Then his eyes shot open, bloodshot and haunted. They saw through George for a moment, lost in the blinding sun before focusing all their rage on the boy. Father grumbled something unintelligible as he clambered to his feet, yanking his pants up to cover his shame. The belt hung from his right hand, wrapped around his palm with the buckle reflecting the sun's light in warning. Once on his feet, Father swayed back and forth as if debating what to do with his son, having wandered in on him like Ham stumbling upon the nakedness of Noah.

George froze for a moment, waiting for his discipline, watching the shimmering buckle swing lazily by his father's feet. The gleam captured George's attention, drawing his gaze to the second pair of feet jutting out from under the hay pile. Cold in their appearance and devoid of color. George recognized them immediately.

"What did you do to her?" George asked, ice in his voice.

"Huh?" His father stepped from the shadow, squinting stupidly. When his mammoth body no longer blocked the view, George saw his Mother splayed on the floor, clothes torn to expose her ravaged body in a way he never wished to see. Dark purple bruising wrapped around her neck in the fashion of a noose, distracting George from her sightless eyes for only a moment.

The story unraveled. Father returning from the saloon at an ungodly hour. Mama trying to keep him from George's room, leading him away from the house. Their all-too familiar, if not quite consensual, routine grew out of hand, and this was the result. And the fucking bastard didn't even remember doing it. A voice spoke from the back of George's mind. Change nothing and nothing changes.

He threw himself at his father, easily outweighed, but not letting it slow him down. Father raised an elbow to stave off George's attack, knocking the boy to the ground with a dulled thud. Dust flew up around him, begging him to stay down. Play dead. But anger clouded George's better judgment. He burst from a prone position, scratching and biting at exposed skin. The salty taste of blood filled his mouth and his father let loose a primitive bellow, not unlike a branded cow. George wrenched his head from side-to-side, trying to cause as much damage as possible until an open palm the size of a pig's head blindsided him across the face and returned him to the ground from whence he came.

George spat and felt a tooth pass through his lips. Before he could throw himself at his father once more, the man raised his right arm and slung the belt down with a mighty force. It slashed through George's shirt and tore into his chest. He wailed as he tried to cover the open wound with both hands. Eyes squeezed shut, George heard the whoosh of the belt before it cleaved into his bicep, slicing through skin and ripping down to the muscle. George screamed his throat raw. He rolled around as if trying to put a fire out and his arm burned as he felt the buckle tear free.

George lifted his trembling hands to cover his face, afraid the next blow might strike there, but after a moment of thrashing and writhing, nothing happened. Risking a peek, he surveyed his father standing over him, stock still and so wide-eyed, George thought he might've been privy to the Lord's return. Sweat poured from the massive man's brow and the front of his pants had gone dark with foul-smelling piss.

"What the fuck?" George rolled to safety and came to rest against the feet of Merella. Her black shawl brought with it the essence of night even in full daylight, emphasizing her pale white skin. She held her left hand perfectly still while carving intricate designs with her right into the air itself.

She kept her gaze fixed on the dumbfounded form of George's father, locking him in some sort of manic daydream. An illusion.

George wasted no time getting up. A quick scan for weapons revealed nothing until his eyes lit on the belt dangling at his father's side. George's blood still trickled off the pointed buckle. He closed the distance in a single large step and unwrapped the belt from his father's outstretched fingers. As he hoisted himself up the mountainous shoulders, he caught another look at his mother's prostrate form. Murdered by the man who'd vowed to love her, cherish her, take care of her until death parted them.

Rage rekindled in George's eyes as he wrapped the belt around his father's neck, cinching the loop, and dropping to the ground to draw it tight. Whatever fear Merella had planted in the man's mind kept him upright. Even as his eyes darkened, the expression of unbridled terror never left. Not until the light dimmed from them completely. George watched the spark vanish an instant before the behemoth's legs gave out and he toppled to the ground. Even then, George planted his feet against the corpse and continued yanking the belt tight—screaming, cursing, and crying for his life.

Merella dropped the hex and sank to her knees, exhausted. She couldn't even bring herself to comfort George. Still bleeding, he sobbed uncontrollably as he continued tugging on the belt. A moment later, strength deserted him and Merella regained her feet and sauntered over.

"Come and take my hand," she said to the mess of a boy laying in a pile of dirt and blood.

Tongues of flame swallowed the stables and barn, then they began to lick at the house. Eventually, they would consume everything on this soon-to-be uninhabited spit of land. The animals, what few the Holcomb family kept, bleated and squealed as George herded them off in the direction of the closest farm. Most would make it there and lead a rich, full life. At least until someone required a slab of bacon. Some would get picked off by coyotes, but that was just the way of the world.

My God, what a world you love.

When the animals had started on their journey, a lone black foal lingered behind.

"Probably need a horse," he said, grinning at Merella.

"What the hell? Bring him along," she replied.

Hand-in-hand, he set off with Merella toward those beautiful mountains, as the midnight-black horse trotted behind them. Buzzard's Edge held nothing for him. Never had, if he was honest. The only part worth staying for was his mother, and she was gone now. He looked over his shoulder as they started out for the open desert and his heart leaped as the flames grew higher.

"I like to think that's Mama, keeping that flickering flame going one last time to keep the darkness away," he said softly.

Merella squeezed his hand and smiled.

"I wanted to ask you." George looked away. "What'd you make him see at the end there?"

She bit her lip and thought for a beat. "Everyone has a monster."

Her icy blue eyes put the period on that sentence. He didn't need to know anymore. George nodded. "What'll we do next?"

"Oh Georgie, I've gotten by for a long time on my own. We're resilient, you and I. We might have to steal every once in a while, but we'll do just fine."

"Yeah," he said. "Yeah, I reckon you're right."

The mountains loomed in the distance even as the silhouette of the town disappeared against the horizon. George didn't recall the peaks being so far away the last time they were out here.

A NOTE FROM
DARKLIT PRESS

All of us at DarkLit Press want to thank you for taking the time to read this book. Words cannot describe how grateful we are knowing that you spent your valuable time and hard-earned money on our publication. We appreciate any and all feedback from readers, good or bad. Reviews are extremely helpful for indie authors and small businesses (like us). We hope you'll take a moment to share your thoughts on Amazon, Goodreads and/or BookBub.

You can also find us on all the major social platforms including Facebook, Instagram, and Twitter. Our horror community newsletter comes jam-packed with giveaways, free or deeply discounted books, deals on apparel, writing opportunities, and insights from genre enthusiasts.

WANTED

Brennan LaFaro is a horror writer living in southeastern Massachusetts with his wife, two sons, and his hounds. An avid lifelong reader, Brennan also co-hosts the Dead Headspace podcast and is the author of Slattery Falls, the first entry in a trilogy, as well as Last Stay, and the horror western, Noose. You can read his short fiction in various anthologies and find him on Twitter/Instagram at @brennanlafaro or at www.brennanlafaro.com.

For more updates, subscribe to Brennan's monthly newsletter, Postcards From the Falls, at Brennanlafaro.substack.com.

CONTENT WARNINGS

Noose

Gun Violence

Blood and Gore

Murder

Suicide

Come and Take My Hand

Child Abuse

Domestic Abuse

Implied Sexual Abuse

Violence

Murder

Printed in Great Britain
by Amazon